T...

Two P...

Endless ... possibilities...

Bridesmaids Margot Walker and Leigh Vaughn
have a wonderful idea to raise money for their friend's
wedding—putting a basket full of spicy date ideas
up for auction. But who will bid? And what, *exactly,*
will the highest bidder be getting?

Margot is hoping her college crush buys her basket.
Too bad her archenemy, Clint Barrows,
beats him to it....

Leigh doesn't have a buyer in mind
when she creates her auction offering.
Good thing—because even after sharing her basket,
she still has no idea who her admirer really is....

Who knew being in a wedding party
came with *these* kinds of perks?

Don't miss:

**#756 *LEAD ME ON* by Crystal Green
(July 2013)**

and

**#765 *MYSTERY DATE* by Crystal Green
(September 2013)**

Blaze®

Dear Reader,

A "basket date" auction, naughty bridesmaids, steamy autumn nights... These are what my two new Blaze stories are made of!

In the first book of this duet, *Lead Me On* (July 2013), you'll meet Margot Walker, who comes up with the idea of creating a spicy date to auction off to the highest bidder. It's for a good cause, of course. The money raised will help pay for her friend Dani's fairy-tale wedding. What she doesn't bargain for is that her archenemy from college, Clint Barrows, intends to win that basket—and make up for some lost time with her.

In the second story, *Mystery Date* (September 2013), you'll find out about the secret admirer who buys fellow bridesmaid Leigh Vaughn's basket...and the lengths he'll go to give her the ultimate fantasy.

I hope you enjoy both stories. Meanwhile, don't forget to enter the contest at my website, www.crystal-green.com. I also have a blog on the site, and I'm on Twitter (@CrystalGreenMe), so check in frequently for updates on upcoming releases.

All the best,

Crystal Green

Crystal Green

—

Lead Me On

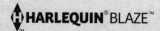

Recycling programs
for this product may
not exist in your area.

ISBN-13: 978-0-373-79760-8

LEAD ME ON

Printed in U.S.A.

ABOUT THE AUTHOR

Crystal Green lives near Las Vegas, where she writes for the Harlequin Special Edition and Blaze lines. She loves to read, overanalyze movies and TV programs, practice yoga, and travel when she can. You can read more about her at www.crystal-green.com, where she has a blog and contests. Also, you can follow her on Twitter @CrystalGreenMe.

Books by Crystal Green

HARLEQUIN BLAZE
261—INNUENDO
303—JINXED!
　　"Tall, Dark & Temporary"
334—THE ULTIMATE BITE
387—ONE FOR THE ROAD
426—GOOD TO THE LAST BITE
472—WHEN THE SUN GOES DOWN
649—ROPED IN

HARLEQUIN SPECIAL EDITION
1850—HER BEST MAN
1887—MOMMY AND THE MILLIONAIRE
1906—THE SECOND-CHANCE GROOM
1932—FALLING FOR THE LONE WOLF
1981—THE TEXAS BILLIONAIRE'S BRIDE
2072—WHEN THE COWBOY SAID I DO
2093—MADE FOR A TEXAS MARRIAGE
2103—TAMING THE TEXAS PLAYBOY

To get the inside scoop on Harlequin Blaze and its talented writers, be sure to check out blazeauthors.com.

Other titles by this author available in ebook format. Don't miss any of our special offers. Write to us at the following address for information on our newest releases.

Harlequin Reader Service
U.S.: 3010 Walden Ave., P.O. Box 1325, Buffalo, NY 14269
Canadian: P.O. Box 609, Fort Erie, Ont. L2A 5X3

To Jolie—your expertise of storytelling and passion for knowledge inspire me!

1

THE VIDEO HAD been posted on YouTube that morning, and Margot Walker was determined to prove that it hadn't bothered her one bit.

So as she sat in a booth in the Avila Grande Suites' bar with her two best friends, she calmly sipped her Midori Sour, leaning back against the leather seat. Around them, conversation buzzed from a few other happy-hour hotel guests—none of whom were a part of the Phi Rho Mu fraternity and Tau Epsilon Gamma sorority ten-year reunion that was taking place in the hotel this weekend.

"Margot," Leigh said, leaning her elbows on the table, her blond braid hanging over a shoulder. "Are you sure you're up for this? Nobody would blame you if you decided to bug out and go home."

Margot carefully set her drink down on the polished table. Dani, with her curly red hair, porcelain skin to die for and a peach-hued shirt, was nodding in agreement beside Leigh.

"Why put yourself through this?"

"Because I'm not going to let a ridiculous prank chase me away," Margot said. "Yes, some bored moron posted that video late last night, hoping to get my goat. Yes, everyone is probably going to laugh at me because of what's on it. But I don't care. No one's keeping me away from meeting up with my friends after all these years."

"You're talking like it's just any old video." Leigh picked up her beer bottle and reclined in her seat, a sexy, laid-back cowgirl in her tight pink-plaid Western shirt. "It was bad enough when it was circulated in college. Now, to have it show up again…?"

"It reflects worse on whoever did this than it does on me," Margot said. And it almost sounded like she believed it.

After all, it *was* humiliating. A dimly lit fraternity room. A couch. Heavy breathing. Her giving in to the one guy she should've never said yes to.

The jerk Clint Barrows.

As Margot pushed a rush of heat back—she was angry, which was why she was blushing and flushing—Dani laughed in amazement.

"That video embarrassed the hell out of you the first time and you never forgave Clint Barrows for it. And don't lie to us, Marg, because we know that's the truth."

"As I said, I got over it." But, when a group of white-collar men wandered into the bar, she momentarily stiffened, waiting to see if she knew them. Waiting to see if they would laugh their asses off at her.

But…no. Just some random guys here on business or whatever.

She forced herself not to hang back in the booth. She was here to show whoever had put up that video that she was an adult, impervious to the slings and arrows of juvenile jokes.

And what a joke it had been. A prank. A camera hidden in a fraternity house during a party one night—the night she'd finally dropped all her hard-to-get flirting with Clint Barrows and given in to his cowboy Romeo charm, going to his room to "watch movies." But movies were the last thing on their minds, and she'd told him that she would kill him if he let anyone know that they were doing anything more than hanging out and eating popcorn.

She hadn't expected to be filmed while saying that and getting hot and heavy with the campus lothario.

Very hot and heavy, although not all-the-way hot and heavy, thank God.

To think, she'd actually liked Clint before she'd gone off with him, had been attracted to him even if he'd had a heck of a lot of women on that secondhand couch and had watched quite a few "movies."

But there was just something about him that had drawn Margot in, even though she'd known he was bad news. Something in his eyes that sparkled dangerously, daring her, inviting her to come on a big adventure she'd never regret. And no guy had ever made her skin tingle with just a look, made her belly flip just at the sound of his voice....

She'd been taken in, though, made sport of. Hunted and caught in the lens of a camera. She'd known it when she'd seen the red eye of the device in the near-dark just as he'd been undoing the buttons on her shirt.

She'd smacked the ever-lovin' charm out of him and left the room, too shocked to even think to destroy the tape. Too... Well, she would've said *hurt* if she'd cared enough.

And she didn't. Really. Because, even when he'd sent an email to her the next morning, telling her that he hadn't known about any camera, that it was his roommate who'd set it up, and that the tape had been demolished, she hadn't answered. Her humiliation had only flared when she'd heard that the video was making the rounds around campus.

Sure, some good sources had backed up Clint's story that he wasn't the one who'd set up or circulated that tape, but when she really thought about it, that wasn't the true reason she couldn't stand him. She'd been caught with him, the conquest king, on film, telling him that their night should be kept a secret. What a laugh riot that must've been for the video's audience before seeing the fireworks that had begun between them.

First off, Margot didn't like being the butt of any joke. Second, she could imagine Clint basking in the glory of the video—proof that he had finally gotten her to bend her will to him. Third, she never wanted to be just a number for *any* guy.

She'd spent college playing hard-to-get for a lot of boys, and her reputation and pride had sure taken a hit after the scandal. And *his* reputation had only grown, his college nickname, "Stud," reaching epic proportions in their social circles for the rest of their senior year.

Her dislike of him had grown with every knowing glance she'd received at every social event after that.

But then summer had come and life had really started. A decade had passed since, and the video had become just one of those ridiculous college mistakes that no one mentioned anymore. It'd been all but forgotten.

Until last night.

Just as she'd been checking her email this morning, all packed and ready to hit the road for this reunion between her sorority and its fraternity counterpart, she'd found messages from her sorority sisters about the video. No one knew who'd posted it, but Margot's first thought went to Clint.

Had he lied about destroying the tape way back then because he thought he could get into her good graces… or her pants…so he could close the deal? And had he aired it now, just because he thought it'd be funny for the reunion?

She wished he'd walk into the bar so she could face him down and tell him to grow up. She was so far beyond him and that night.

As she rested her hand on her glass of Midori Sour, she smiled at her friends. "Why bring that crap up again when we have more important things to talk about? As in, auction baskets for this weekend?"

Leigh caught her cue and shot a glance to Dani. They'd all met in the lobby about fifteen minutes ago and had just sat and started chatting when the scandal had reared its ugly head again. Margot had already told them she was over it on the phone during her drive there, but leave it to Dani and Leigh to question her.

Anyway, when they'd first seen each other, hugging and laughing, she and Leigh had sprung their own surprise on Dani, telling her about the charity auction the two of them were throwing tomorrow night because they wanted her to have the big wedding she'd always yearned for. It'd be an All-American college-reunion good time that wasn't going to be ruined just because some ass—*had* it been Clint?—had decided to pep up the event with a memory Margot would've rather forgotten.

Once again, she thought of the cowboy, with his denim-blue eyes, his lackadaisical way of watching her walk through one of the many parties their fraternity and sorority had thrown together. Then, just as quickly, she tamped down that spark in her belly.

Jerk.

"Guess what I'm going to call my auction basket," she said, ignoring thoughts of him.

Dani was strangely quiet, just as she'd been when Leigh and Margot had launched the surprise on her, come to think of it.

But Leigh was already talking, leaving the video behind, although Margot suspected it'd come up again.

"Lord knows what you conjured up, Marg."

Her smile grew. "'Around the Girl in Eighty Ways.'"

She waited for them to give her that "come again?" look that she'd gotten so used to back in college when she'd whipped up similar harebrained ideas.

And, yep, there it was.

Come again?

Leigh took the bait first. "How does going around the girl in eighty ways fit in an auction basket?"

"I'm betting it'll fit very nicely on auction night. Hopefully even more than once." Margot shot Leigh a saucy grin, while Dani just lifted an eyebrow at Margot.

Then Dani said, "I'm not sure about all this…."

Leigh nudged Dani good-naturedly. "You've got to hear Margot out. She came down here, even in the midst of a pride-spankin', just for you, Dan."

"Thanks," Margot said, narrowing her eyes at Leigh. She spoke to Dani. "This is just the first of many gifts for our bride-to-be."

"But I don't need—"

"It's not a matter of need or not need," Margot said, on a roll. See—it wasn't so hard to forget about that video. Sort of. "You used to talk about the perfect wedding all the time. *Everyone* wants it to happen for you at the end of this year in the huge, grand way you used to describe to us."

"You were our Wedding Girl," Leigh added, giving Dani's arm a friendly, light squeeze.

Dani said nothing, and Margot caught Leigh's gaze. Sure, they'd talked about whether or not they were being too intrusive, assuming Dani would want their help, since her funds were too low to afford that dream wedding. But, my God, this was *Dani*. And this was their chance to help her achieve the fantasies she'd collected in her wedding scrapbook—pictures of frothy white dresses and creamy cakes, blooming flowers and a bride and groom who couldn't take their eyes off each other.

If someone good like Dani didn't deserve it all, then who did?

"You've already talked about this auction to everyone?" Dani finally asked.

Across the table, Leigh looked a little sheepish as she put down her beer. "We might've secretly suggested it to the sisters on our email loop."

Dani was flushing, and Margot wasn't sure if she was embarrassed or angry with them. But Dani never got angry.

When she spoke, she made Margot rethink that.

"So everyone knows that poor me, the lowly caterer and not the Paula Deen she aimed to be back when she majored in home ec, can't afford a decent wedding? And her fiancé is only a small-estate manager, not the business mogul he wanted to become, so that means they can't possibly afford even fancy flower arrangements?" She laughed. "I suppose that's not too embarrassing."

Margot glanced at Leigh again. *Whoops*.

Leigh seemed just as helpless as Margot as she peeled away the label of her beer. "Can I just put things in perspective and volunteer that Margot's video is going to take all the 'embarrassing' out of the reunion for you, Dan? That's what everyone'll be talking about."

To Leigh's credit, she was merely doing her best. Margot followed suit.

"Once again, Leigh, thanks so much." She smiled at Dani. "No one thinks you're destitute. It's only that your wedding plans were legendary in the sorority. Hell, your nickname during pledging was 'Hearts.' We'd talk about getting together for the ceremony someday and how it'd be a time when we could all celebrate together."

"It was going to be a milestone," Leigh added.

Margot went on, and it was just like the old days, when she would get a lightbulb idea going and Leigh would join in, eventually followed by Dani.

"The wedding is as much for us as it is for you," she said. "It means everything because you're marrying the guy from our counterpart fraternity, and everyone knew you were going to get together with him even before the two of you knew it. It's a big deal for all of us Rhos and Taus."

Dani finally smiled, probably because of the memories.

Times like the spring-break trip to Cabo—a Bacchanalia that had sworn Margot, Leigh and Dani off booze for…well, weeks. It had been just one of many adventures they'd shared as sorority sisters and Margot would never forget them. The three of them had grown up together during some very pivotal years, then tossed their graduation caps in the air as one, letting them rain down with the joy of exploring all the roads ahead.

Back then, Margot had nursed so many ambitions— to travel the world, to write books—and she'd done *all* of it in the time from there to here.

But dreams could last only so long.

She ate the maraschino cherry in her Midori Sour, yet it didn't taste as good as it used to—not after the bad news she'd gotten last month about how her latest "single girl on the go" travel book had done.

Or, more to the point, *hadn't* done.

As usual, Margot tried not to show how upset she was. She'd been keeping the news to herself that her publishing company hadn't wanted to go to contract after she closed out this most recent book. Surely something else was bound to come along.

Wouldn't it?

Dani was talking. "But…I still don't know about raising money for my wedding."

Leigh said, "Don't they have money dances at receptions? We'd just be doing the asking *before* the wedding."

"Besides, it's not any old auction," Margot was quick to add, dangling the cherry stem between her fingers. "This is something everyone will love. A basket auction, just like they used to do in the old days at picnics. You know, when the girls packed a lunch in a basket and tied a telltale ribbon around the handle so the boy she was crushing on would know it was hers and take her out?"

"Days of innocence," Leigh said in her ranch-girl drawl. Country-singer cool, she rested her free arm over the top of the booth. She seemed as down-to-earth as they came—if you didn't know her very well. Leigh was the type to come off as earthy, even though she was a rising star at The Food Network with a new show that Margot could describe only as "sensuous farmhouse cooking"—like putting Faith Hill in Martha Stewart's kitchen.

For a second, Margot could almost see her friends as they used to be: Leigh, forty pounds heavier, laughing at the nickname—"Cushions"—that everyone had given her, even while inside, Margot knew, Leigh hadn't found it so hilarious. And Dani, a home ec major like Leigh, known as the romantic "Hearts," who used to love matchmaking at the dinner parties she put together.

But Margot had them beat. She'd been an endangered species on their rural San Joaquin Valley campus— an English major among all the agricultural business majors and local cowboys and cowgirls. She'd never minded standing out, though. Leigh, who'd been her dorm roomie, and Dani, who'd lived down the hall, had talked Margot into joining Tau Epsilon Gamma, and she'd never regretted a day of it.

Even if her parents hadn't been quite as excited.

Sororities are for girls who'll never find a day of independence in their lives, her dad had said. *Don't you want to have a mind of your own?*

Of course she did, but joining the Taus hadn't quashed the free spirit her hippy-minded parents had raised her to be as they'd moved from town to town, "experiencing all life has to offer." They'd take temporary jobs and then one day jerk her out of school before she could find a best friend. Sometimes she'd wondered if they cared about how she fit into their whole "see the world!" philosophy…or if she'd just been one more item on their bucket lists.

But she'd found a whole lot of friends all on her own, thank you very much.

And *that's* what mattered.

Margot searched Dani's gray-hued gaze. Was her friend about to come around to the idea of the auction? She and Leigh hadn't meant to mortify her; when

Dani had told them during their own private yearly get-together a few months ago that she and Riley couldn't afford the wedding she'd been planning since she was a little girl, it'd looked as if her heart was about to break.

Or was Dani going to tell them to go to hell?

"Dani," Margot said, reaching across the table to enclose her hand, which rested by her untouched wine spritzer. "We can call off the auction if you want. Really."

Leigh looked as if she was holding her breath, clearly just as torn about this. Since she'd lost weight last year, she'd made a pact with Margot to be more adventurous than ever. Hence, this basket thing. Even though she'd always seemed confident, she hadn't been anywhere near it. Now, though, Leigh was different, and she was going to take her new attitude into the bedroom for the very first time in her life with this auction. She'd vowed to do things like making love with the lights on and playing all the bedroom games she'd never allowed herself to play.

And Margot… Well, *she* was pretty much already one of those girls, never settling into a relationship, since there was so much to do out in the world, so much to see and experience. Putting together a sinful basket would be one more adventure for the adventuress—and it'd be a way to say "See? That damned YouTube video isn't going to cow me" to whoever had posted it.

Clint?

Truthfully, there was a bonus in the basket auction. This weekend would also be a chance to reconnect with her old boyfriend, Brad, maybe relive some good old times….

Margot stopped herself. These days, *she* wasn't as

confident as everyone thought. She felt like a real fail-ure at the moment, with her less-than-bestselling books.

Most Likely to Succeed?

Not so much anymore. But she was damned if she was going to let anyone see the self-doubt. Nope—she had taken the lead in putting together this auction, and she wanted it to go off without a hitch, video or no. She would do it for Dani's sake and…

Well, to let everyone know that nothing was going to get her down.

"Dani?" Leigh asked. "Do you want us to cancel the auction?"

A second passed, and Margot maintained her poker face, even as her heart beat against her ribs.

But then Dani smiled. "I'd hate to ruin anyone's fun…."

"I knew you'd be on board," Leigh said, beaming.

Margot raised her drink, even though she thought she still detected some reluctance in Dani. "To a hell of an auction, then?"

"I'll drink to that." Leigh toasted, too. "Then again, I've got the feeling we'll be drinking to a lot of *thats* this weekend."

Dani brought her spritzer glass up as well, and they all clinked, then threw their drinks down the hatch.

When they finished, Margot noticed that the room was filling up. Businessmen cluttered the mahogany bar, loosening their ties and glancing around.

When the waitress stopped by to check on the three women, Leigh ordered another round of drinks. Then the server went to the next booth, the occupant obscured by the strip of stained glass edging the top of the seats.

Obviously, someone had slipped in, unnoticed, during their conversation, because the waitress took that order, too. Couldn't be anyone they knew, Margot thought, or they would've said hi.

"So, Margot," Leigh began, "how about that Around the Girl in Eighty Ways basket?"

"What, are you going to steal ideas from me?" Margot asked playfully.

"Like I'd need to."

They'd always tried to top each other in grades and at social events, and they'd made each other challenge themselves, too, Margot thought. Too bad she didn't have Leigh around more these days.

She brushed off the pessimism. There wasn't room for it this weekend. "The title pretty much says it all, doesn't it? I have little pieces of paper with different… scenarios…on them. Whoever bids the highest can enact one or more of them during our date."

"Whoa," Leigh said. "Brassy. I thought I'd make mine a little vaguer, you know? Just in case it goes to someone who doesn't really appeal."

"Oh, I'm going to make sure it goes to someone who appeals to me. But not to worry—the scenarios I've chosen can be interpreted in various ways. They can be as naughty as I want…or as nice."

"You devil," Leigh said.

"Or angel." Margot winked and took another drink.

"Just exactly what kind of scenarios are they?" Dani asked.

Behind them, in the other booth, someone cleared his throat.

Margot barely heard, because she was concentrating on Dani. She loved to see that her friend was warming to this basket idea. "*Scenarios.* You know me. My books were all about seeking fun for the well-traveled girl, so I've got several adventures already researched and tested."

She hesitated. Her books *were* all about seeking fun? Had she really just used the past tense?

Leigh's olive-colored eyes lit up. "I can see where this is going."

"Can you?"

"Please, Marg," Dani said. "Even a few months ago, you were talking about seeing Brad here at the reunion. I think we can figure out that you're going to make sure *he's* the one who bids the highest, so you can rekindle that flame you had in junior summer break."

"Did you tell him about your basket yet?" Leigh asked.

Margot thought that she could finally taste a hint of the thick, decadent juice that had come with the mara-schino cherry. "I had no idea that Brad was going to be here," she said, all sweetness and cluelessness.

"Right," Dani said.

"As if you didn't know he got divorced recently," Leigh added.

He was the only guy Margot had connected with in a half-serious way. Okay, the relationship had lasted only about three months, during a summer when he'd taken off from Cal-U and interned on a local dairy near Chico, where she'd been staying with a cousin during break. But he'd lit her teenage fire on more than one occasion.

What she'd give for a little of that fire now.

She glanced around to see if any of her classmates had noticed she was here yet.

Dani cleared her throat. "Riley told me he heard Brad's going to break away from work this weekend. He'll be here, all right."

Leigh waggled her eyebrows. "You plan to have a special mark on your basket so he can bid on it?"

"A burst of gold and silver stars." Margot smiled at the waitress as she brought the new round of drinks.

Leigh murmured, "A burst of stars, just like he'll see after Margot—"

She cut Leigh off. "When did Riley say Brad was coming, Dan?"

"I think he's here already, playing golf with Riley and some of the guys before things really get started."

Everyone would be here by tomorrow for the homecoming football game, then a casual meal and the auction, followed on Sunday by a more formal dinner before they all headed off in their different directions again.

Leigh leaned back in the booth, surveying Margot. "Honestly, I never really saw Brad's appeal. He always reminded me of the type of guy who checks himself out in windows when he walks by them. He was kind of self-involved, if you ask me."

"He was not." He was smart and ambitious, going places. Margot had related to that. Plus, he'd been in the area, and they'd gotten to know each other without all their Greek brothers and sisters around.

Dani was leaning her elbows on the table, looking at Leigh. "I never thought Brad was that hot, either."

Hot?

The word conjured up a maddening image of Clint Barrows. That damn video had shoved him into her mind and was making him stay there beyond a decent hello. God, she hoped he wouldn't be at the reunion.

Margot took another drink, as if she could wash him away.

Dani started to slide out of the booth. "Don't hate

me, but I'm really bushed, you all. I catered a big for-
tieth birthday party last night. Can we meet up later?"

When Margot started to protest, Leigh stood to leave,
too. "Don't hate *me,* but I've got a script to look over
and approve tonight so we can hit the ground running
at the studio on Monday."

"Lightweights," Margot muttered. She wasn't nearly
ready to hole up in her room yet, even if her classmates
would soon be here to tease her about the video.

Bring them on.

Leigh seemed impressed. "You're actually staying
here?"

"To face the lions when they arrive? You'd better believe it. I want to get this over with. Besides, if Brad's
already in town, he might drop in for a post-golf drink."

"Okay, Braveheart." Leigh smiled. "How about dinner with us later?"

"No doubt."

Dani just grinned again, swinging her small, patch-
work purse over her shoulder. They both waved as they
walked away, and it wasn't four seconds later that Margot started rethinking this Braveheart stuff.

Did she really want to suffer through the ribbing
all alone?

But it wasn't in her nature to wimp out, so she took
another drink.

A deep voice behind her made her almost spray the
Midori out of her mouth.

"I've always wondered what'd be in your basket."

She knew that voice, even years later.

Clint Freakin' Barrows.

2

INEXPLICABLY, A DELICIOUS shiver danced up Margot's back, just like fingers running over bare skin then stopping at her neck, stroking until the fine hairs stood on heated end. And that wasn't the only part of her body that responded; she went tight nearly everywhere, from her sensitized nipples to the clenching of her belly.

She also felt a sharp ache between her legs, but she chased it away.

She blew out a breath, wishing her stomach wasn't all scrambled. Then she turned around to find the one and only Clint Barrows leaning off the edge of the bench seat, his arms resting on his thighs, his cowboy hat tipped back on his head.

A slow melt started inside her as she took in his grin. This wasn't the college kid she remembered. Not exactly. The Clint Barrows who'd lured her to his room that one night had been cute—no doubts there—but now?

Now he had shoulders *this* wide under his white T-shirt. And his thighs hadn't been so muscular under faded jeans. And there was some age to him—smile lines around his light blue eyes and hair that seemed to be an even thicker golden mess under his hat.

Like a fine bourbon, he'd aged well.

Damn him for looking so good. Damn her for feeling a little dizzy just from standing near him.

How…after all these years…?

And, after what he'd done?

"You've got some gall," she said.

He laughed. "Because I'm saying hi?"

She just stared at him. Talk about thickheaded.

"Darlin'," he said, clearly knowing that she was talking about the video. "Don't go accusing me of anything. First off, I don't have the time to be digging through old videos and sharing them with the world. Second, I destroyed that tape."

"Well, then, I guess it magically came to life again and found itself a cozy home on YouTube. You're in the clear, *Stud.*"

He laughed once more, smooth and low, and her clit gave a vicious little twist.

Oh, come on—she hadn't gone without a man *that* long. Or maybe she had. Now that she thought about it, it'd been months. She'd been locked away, pounding out a draft of her most recent book, which had given her more trouble than most. The wildness and joy just didn't come as easily as it used to. Maybe that's why her book sale numbers were going down….

She lifted a finger at him. "If you're not here to rub that video in, then why did you show up? I didn't think reunions would be your scene."

"Just call it a last-minute decision."

Cryptic, and so Clint Barrows. And with that grin of his, she wanted to solve whatever mystery he was putting out there.

Or did she?

"Come on," he said. "Why don't you just sit down and talk about this."

"Are you kidding? *First,* I don't believe your story. *Second,* I think we'll get along much better if I'm on one side of the room and you're on the other."

He sighed. "Have it your way, then. For now."

For now?

Shaking her head, she grabbed her Fendi purse and got out the hand-worked leather wallet she'd bought in Florence once upon a time. Earlier, she'd told the girls she would be taking care of the bar tab, even though she wasn't sure she could afford many flights of generosity like this in the future.

"So about those baskets…" Clint said.

Once a tease, always a tease.

"Don't even start."

"Start what? If you recall, there're things I start that you have a problem ending."

"See? Rubbing it in. I knew you wouldn't be able to resist."

"Give me a chance here, Shakespeare."

Her libido gave another hot jerk. She'd liked how he used to call her English author names the few times they'd actually talked during parties. He'd amused her—and she'd been turned on that a cowboy had known his literature, to tell the truth.

But that was before she'd found out he'd only wanted to set her up for an adolescent joke.

"You think this is all so funny," she said.

He sobered and, for a second, she thought he was actually being sincere.

"I don't think it's a bit funny. But—"

She slapped her cash on the table and left, even while

every cell in her body was pulling her toward his booth, vibrating with the curiosity she hadn't been able to fully appease on that long-ago night.

But if there was one thing Margot would guard until the end, it was pride.

Luckily, that's when she heard her name being called from the other side of the bar.

A group of fraternity brothers, including Dani's fiancé, Riley, had just walked in, and she recognized her ex-boyfriend Brad among them.

Or, at least, she thought she did.

He looked like one of the businessmen at the bar—creased khakis and a crisp, long-sleeved shirt. His dark hair was neatly trimmed, unlike a certain cowboy's that looked as if he turned tail and ran every time a barber came near.

Brad lifted a hand in greeting to her, giving her a friendly smile. He didn't seem to care about the video. None of them did, maybe because Riley had told them to back off during their golf game.

Margot waved back, then waited for the rush of heat to swamp her horny body, just as it had with Clint.

Waiting…

Waiting…

It only happened again when she heard Clint's voice behind her.

"You'd best go to Brad," he said. "Good ol' dependable Brad…."

She felt Brad watching her from across the room, and she didn't want to give him the impression that she was taking up where she'd left off in that video with Clint Barrows.

"You can walk away now," Clint said. "But I'll be seeing you later."

"Dare to dream," she said over her shoulder.

And she left him with that, his laughter skimming across her skin, heating her to blazing for no good reason she could think of.

Except for the million and one tongues of flame licking at her, daring her to turn around and scratch the itch that'd never quite gone away.

CLINT WATCHED HER leave, enjoying the sway of her hips beneath her tight pants, which were tucked into high boots, giving her the kind of flair you'd normally see with a hoity-toity princess out for a ride on an English saddle.

He'd always been a legs and ass man and, thanks to those clothes, both were on cock-teasing display with Margot Walker.

She got to him in a lot of ways, with her long, layered dark brown hair that was somehow classy and gypsylike at the same time. With pale sea-hued eyes that always seemed to be shining with a sense of humor that also came out in her carefree laugh. Her delicate features—a slightly turned-up nose, high cheekbones, a heart-shaped face—reminded him of one of the wood fairy figurines that his mom used to keep on the top shelf in the family room. Statues that had stayed there even years after she'd died, when Clint was just learning to break in horses.

Dignified, delicate, yet slightly wild. That was Margot Walker to a T.

Something fisted in his gut, reminding him of how much he'd wanted her ten years ago. The smart girl who knew how to put down the books and have fun. The life of every party, who lit up a room just by walking into it.

And that was the exact reason he'd been over the

moon when she'd come up to his room with him that night.

The thing of it was, he'd genuinely been aiming to watch a movie with her, since they'd been chatting about *The Untouchables* down at the party and he'd owned a copy.

Her willingness to be alone with him had stunned him, because Margot had always seemed untouchable herself, the only girl who never gave him the time of day…until she'd let down her guard in his room.

At first, he'd sat a decent distance from her on that Naugahyde couch. But, slowly, they'd gotten closer, as if attraction had pulled them together like magnets. And by the time Kevin Costner and Andy Garcia went to the train station to intercept a witness for their case against Al Capone, his gaze was on Margot, not the screen.

And she had been watching him, too, with a softness in her eyes he'd never seen before.

"God help you if you tell anyone about this," she said before they'd come together.

He'd never been swept away by a girl before, but this one night, it'd happened. And as they kissed— her breath in his ear as she whispered his name—he'd thought that this was it. Margot Walker was the one woman who could make him think there was no one else, just as his dad had thought the same about his mom when they were both alive.

Then, unbeknownst to him, she'd seen the camera, and before he could ask what had gotten her so upset, she'd slapped him, pulled her shirt together, angry as hell, and bolted out of the room without telling him what was wrong.

As confused as he was, he hadn't gone after her.

And he hadn't noticed the camera hidden in the corner.

Soon afterward, he'd gone back down to the party to see if she was still there, but she'd left him in the dust, wondering what he'd done.

It wasn't until the next morning, when his roommate, Jay Halverson, the fraternity historian, couldn't hold it in any longer, that he found out what'd happened: Jay had seen Clint downstairs, making inroads with the one girl who'd always eluded him. He'd bet that Clint would pull through and bring her back to his room and that the moment should be recorded for the brotherhood's posterity.

Clint's blood had been boiling, but when Jay had cued up the video and shown it to him, they'd come to blows. As collateral damage, the video was decimated, smashed to pieces.

But it didn't matter, because Jay had already made a copy and had given it to some of his friends to watch.

Of course, Margot had sent Clint an email about it that night but he hadn't seen the message until after the fight with Jay. The content was curt and crisp, barely hiding the hurt that he knew she must've felt. He'd written back that he'd destroyed the tape, leaving out the part where Jay had actually been the one who'd filmed her. But she never answered.

Especially after the video made its way from the TV of one fraternity member to the next.

The copy was never found and, for more reasons than the video, Jay was eventually blackballed. But that didn't give Clint another chance with Margot. It didn't make him forget her, either, as he ran the cutting horse ranch he loved just a half hour away from Avila Grande, California, and their alma mater.

As he sat in that booth now, watching her walk to Brad, he thought how sad it was that he'd actually come to understand why Margot had reacted the way she did: she didn't intend to be just an item on a list, or a person a man would forget when he moved on to the next girl. She'd never been merely one of the crowd, and she'd gone out and proved it to the world with that sophisticated career of hers.

And she hadn't wanted to be the fool, caught on tape as Clint "conquered" her.

Who would?

Seeing her today, a disturbingly hot woman who grabbed him and twisted him inside out, Clint was fascinated all over again. Not that she'd given him the chance to explain, but he'd come to this reunion for one reason and one reason only.

To set matters straight and make it up to her.

He hadn't planned on coming, not when there was so much going on with his younger twin brothers and the ranch. But when he'd been told the video had found new life on YouTube, he'd blown a gasket, immediately sending an email to his fraternity brothers saying that if they razzed Margot about it this weekend, they'd answer to him.

So far, it looked like they were respecting his requests. Margot stood at the bar with Brad Harrington, laughing and pushing a hank of that stylish gypsy hair away from her face. She was saying hi to the group that had just walked into the dark-wooded room. From this distance, it was pretty obvious that Brad was being amiable enough, but...

Could it be that he wasn't really in to her?

Nah. Clint couldn't imagine a red-blooded male

anywhere within the boundaries of the U.S. of A. who wouldn't be eating up her charms.

As Clint toyed with his shot glass, one man broke away from the crowd and moved toward the booth. Clint nodded in greeting to Riley Donahue, then stood to shake his hand just as the waitress came with the other whiskies he'd ordered.

"Took you long enough to get here," Clint said.

"We were having too much fun. You should've come with us."

"Golf's not my game." Again, he stole a glance at Margot, who'd taken a seat on a bar stool and was leaning toward Brad. From here, he could see her sweater gaping open, revealing a gut-punching hint of black bra. Her breasts were round and full, pressed into smooth globes by the tight lace.

He could feel himself getting hard, and he pulled his gaze away. "How's the life of a happy bachelor?" he asked Riley instead.

Riley, who'd also pledged with Clint and become a good friend, ran a hand through his short black hair. "Happy? I guess you must not have heard the news."

He wasn't talking about getting married, seeing as Riley and Dani had been engaged for about a year. They'd been friends until they'd "awakened," or some such greeting-card crap, one day and really "seen" each other.

Fairy tales, Clint thought. His parents had had a lot of great years together, but it'd just never happened for him. Then again, it wasn't as if he'd ever wanted to settle down. He'd grown up as a lone wolf while his brothers had depended on each other, forming their own inner circle and keeping him out, and he'd been the same way with everyone else, especially women.

The true love of his life had always been the ranch—
a paradise invaded by twin snakes, aka his own flesh-
and-blood siblings. Funny how he'd found much better
brothers, like Riley, away at college.

Clint made himself comfortable in the booth. "Oh,
I've certainly heard the news. I've already heard more
than I bargained for about the auction."

Margot telling Dani and Leigh about her basket…
The sparkly stars that would be a sure sign that it was
hers…

But she meant the damn thing for someone else, so
why was he even dwelling on it?

*Because there are definitely at least eighty ways you
could get around her,* he thought. And he could guarantee that she enjoyed every one of them, making up
lost time with her.

Saying sorry about that tape in every way he could.

Riley spoke, his voice edged with mild frustration.
"The guys were all over me about this auction when we
were playing golf. I guess the girls' email loop got everyone talking before we got here and Dani didn't know
it. Nothing like finding out that everyone is swimming
in your personal business. I damn well hope Dani put
an end to it this afternoon."

"From what I hear, the girls just want Dani to have
that wedding she always planned for. No harm, no foul."

"I already feel like shit that I can't give that wedding
to Dani myself, and to have us turn into some kind of
charity case…?" He shook his head.

From what Clint had overheard, Dani hadn't asked
Margot and Leigh to call off the auction. But—

Sparkling stars… Around the Girl in Eighty Ways…

Riley interrupted. "Ever since I heard about that auction, I've wanted to tell Dani that I'd rather elope to a

Vegas chapel. But then I think about how much she's always talked about the dress with one of those long trains or whatever they call it, and how she wants things to happen in a big church with a big reception, and…I just lose the words."

Clint signaled for yet another round. Riley sure looked like he needed it. Honestly, Clint could use some more drinks, too, because every time he glanced at Margot across the room canoodling with Brad, he felt a keen urge to water down.

"What're you going to tell Dani, then?" Clint asked. "I think the sisters who keep in touch on email are looking forward to this auction."

And he was, too?

But that was idiotic, because that basket of Margot's was aimed at Brad. Plus, she wanted Clint on one side of the room and her on another.

He was damned sure going to change her mind about that.

Riley blew out a breath. "I know Margot and Leigh went to a lot of work. *Everyone* who brought a basket did, and their intentions are good."

"Then let everyone play. You can tell the sisters that you're not taking a dime and the proceeds can go to a charity."

Riley's head jerked up, and he looked at Clint as if he were a genius. Yeah, well, he would be about the only one to think that.

But Clint wasn't here to dwell on the troubles back on the ranch, not when he was among people who'd been even closer to him for a time than his own family. He hadn't ever thought that his relationship with the twins could get worse, except it had, a couple years ago, when Dad had passed on and split up his estate, giving Clint

60 percent of the cutting horse ranch and Jeremiah and Jason each 20 percent. It made all the sense in the world to Clint, who'd come back home after getting his agriculture business degree and developed the Circle BBB, while the twins had opted for the city and an agriculture development firm they'd built from the ground up.

Things never changed, and the twins still stuck together like glue. According to them, Clint didn't know what he was doing with the ranch, even though he ran a solid and profitable operation. But, with their business experience "out in the world," they thought they knew better.

"Why don't you just drink on this auction business," he said to Riley, raising his shot glass.

They slammed back their whisky, then bolted their glasses to the table.

As the waitress slid another round to them and left, Clint's gaze inevitably fixed on Margot again. By now, she was resting her hand on Brad's arm as they shared another joke.

Clint threw back the newest shot. He kept telling himself Brad was his fraternity brother. Brad was making her laugh when she needed it, which was more than Clint had accomplished earlier.

Riley was rolling up his sleeves, as if acknowledging it was going to be a long-ass reunion weekend. Then he noticed the direction of Clint's gaze, and he followed it out the booth and over his shoulder, spying Margot.

He turned back to Clint, holding back a grin. "Got your email about the video this morning. Still have some feelings for her?"

"Not even a speck." He was pissed that it was so obvious. "I just figured it'd be proper to do some damage control for her sake."

"Right." Riley fiddled with his glass. "Was Jay the one who posted that video?"

"It appears so. He runs his family's farm now, so I got a hold of him there. He took the video down already."

"Did you threaten to cuff him again?"

"No. I just did what my brothers do and I threw a few legal words around. That did the trick."

"Why'd he even post it?"

"He said it was his contribution to the reunion, but you remember Jay well enough. He was bitter after we blackballed him for not paying dues and—"

"In general being a douche bag."

"That, too." Clint pushed his glass away. "Him posting the video was nothing against Margot, but it sure feels personal."

Riley paused, making Clint shift in his seat. No use lying about how interested he still was in Margot.

"Just a warning," Riley said. "Dani will even tell you that Margot is still as hard to get as ever."

Now Clint's pride was poked, and dammit, it'd been happening too much lately for him to tolerate it.

"She may be hard to get," he said, "but not impossible."

"Good luck, after what happened last night with the video."

"She'll put it behind her."

"Whoa. Is that a challenge I hear?"

Clint smiled, then jerked his chin toward the bar. Margot sat right next to Brad, arm to arm.

God.

He glanced away, not wanting to watch, but clearly unable to help himself.

"Not that I want to encourage you," Riley said, "because I think she's a lost cause, but Brad doesn't seem all that interested in her. I remember way back when he dated Margot that summer and it didn't work out."

Clint's smile was back. "Why do you think that was?"

"You know Brad. His parents were conservative as hell and raised him to marry a girl who'd be a good wife. Margot was just a fling while he was interning far from home and both of them probably knew it wouldn't go anywhere. Besides, he got divorced a few months ago, and he's a long way from dating anyone again." Riley picked up his next glass. "But if your mind is set on Margot, I'll be your wingman. Dani knows that you're not really the guy with the bad reputation you got because of some college joke. I don't know why you never stressed to Margot that Jay was behind it all."

"Wouldn't have done any good. She'd already written me off."

"So why do you think things will change now?"

"Just a hunch."

Clint glanced at the ill-fated couple. Brad leaned his elbow on the bar instead of canting toward Margot, his disinterest clearer than shiny glass.

Maybe things would work out, he thought.

Maybe he *would* get to make everything up to her.

3

So far, everyone had treated the subject of the video as if it was no big deal, and that gave Margot quite the shot of joy. Why had she even been worried? They were all way past college mischief.

But she couldn't ignore how some of the brothers, as well as Brad, kept glancing over at Clint. Even if they weren't teasing her about that video, it was on everyone's mind.

Just one more reason to avoid him.

She'd actually been working up to telling Brad about her basket for the past hour, but things were still a little haven't-seen-you-in-a-long-time tense between them. Still, he hadn't dropped any hints about having a girlfriend or anything.

So why not go forward?

She ran a gaze from his wavy dark brown hair to his smile. He'd always reminded her of Ben Affleck but much less cocksure...unlike another person she could name.

But she wasn't going to think of Kid Quick-Trigger on the other side of the room, in his booth, drinking whiskey. Mr. I'm-So-Cool-in-a-Cowboy-Hat. Señor Slick. She'd been telling herself to ignore Clint Barrows over and over, but this time she meant it.

Brad set his beer down on the bar. It was still half-full. "It really is good to see you, Margot."

Did she hear a "but…" in there somewhere?

"I liked seeing you, too," she said. "Catching up has been nice."

Was *nice* the word for the conversation they'd been having about running a dairy farm?

Then again, was her auction basket all about the art of conversation?

He fiddled with his beer mug for a moment, then said, "Some of us are getting up early tomorrow to go fishing. Don't ask me why we torture ourselves like this."

"Why do you?" She smiled, hoping to get past this semi-awkward stage and right to the basket.

"Because that's what we used to do," he said. "Fish. Golf. Be sportsmen." He checked his silver watch, then got out his wallet to pay the bar tab. "I'll see you tomorrow at the homecoming pregame kegger?"

He was…leaving?

Margot's Girl Survival Mode kicked into gear, telling her this was a bad time to blurt out that, hey, she'd really like to spend some private, quality sex time with him, and by the way, here's what her basket would look like tomorrow evening at the auction, because she really, truly thought they could have quite the reunion all by themselves.

One more adventure, right?

But, ever since she'd gotten the news from her publisher, she'd started to wonder if, after college, she had set out to have adventures on her own only because experiences filled a hole that'd been put there by never having a true home. Had she been trying to find one by going from place to place, person to person, just as her parents had before they'd passed on eight years ago?

And…her parents. It's not like they'd taught her about a whole lot besides "loving life" and "smelling the roses along the primrose path." Sometimes, she even wondered if they'd loved her half as much as all their pleasure-seeking activities. One time, they had even turned a room in the two-bedroom house they'd been renting into an art studio for their projects, and she'd had to sleep on the couch. She'd been eight.

The thoughts dogged her, even as she started to get the vibe that things weren't gelling with Brad.

He rested a companionable hand on her shoulder and squeezed it, then started to leave the bar. "See you later, Marg."

As he left, she tried not to let hurt set in. She was usually much better at this, distancing herself before anyone could do it to her first.

She just sat there as he disappeared, wondering why Brad's attitude didn't hurt more.

She decided to go, too, and she thought she felt Clint's gaze tracking her out the door. Then it occurred to her… Even though Brad hadn't teased her about the video, had it made him look at her differently?

As used goods, viewed by hundreds of people sitting in front of a computer?

It didn't matter anyway, because she'd blown her chance to tell Brad about her basket so he could bid on it.

On her way into the lobby, she came to a dead stop. What was with her? She'd always taken charge. It was what a single girl did.

At least, the type she used to be.

Full of determination, she went to the reception desk, asked for paper and an envelope, then scribbled a note, since the clerk wouldn't release a room number that she could call.

Brad,
I didn't get the chance to broach the subject, but I'd love to get together before the weekend's over. If you're interested, you could always bid on the basket with the silver and gold stars attached to the handle. It might bring back a few adventurous memories…or make a few new ones.

It wasn't like her to hesitate, but she definitely did when she reread that last part.

Ah, screw it. Adventure!

She signed her name, stuffed the note into the hotel envelope, then generously tipped the concierge and asked him to deliver it to Brad. She liked this much more mysterious way to approach him rather than just calling him up. It was part of the basket's seduction.

Feeling much better, she took a detour outside to the parking lot, to her Prius, where her bags were still in the trunk. She had arrived before her room was ready and met Leigh and Dani right after checking in.

The night was mid-October-crisp, with the scent of wood smoke in the air. Avila Grande, home of Cal-U, was near Route 99, and she could hear the faint swish of cars traveling along it. In high school, she'd loved John Steinbeck's work—what could she say about the streak of Americana in her?—and when Cal-U had offered her a scholarship for their fledgling English program, she'd snapped it up.

But being here now felt a little lonely, and she tried not to sink into the mire of her thoughts again—the voice of her literary agent telling her that it didn't look likely that she would be picked up by her publishing house anytime in the near future. She fought back the looming question of where her paychecks would be coming from after her royalties dried up and her savings had been gutted.

This weekend was supposed to be about Dani, but maybe also about thinking of a new direction for herself, right? So why wasn't she feeling brave?

When she heard boot steps on the pavement, she slammed down her trunk and set her bags on the blacktop. She'd taken Krav Maga, and she was always ready to use it.

"Whoa," said a familiar male voice that made shivers sweep up and down her skin.

She went tight all over again—in her belly, then lower, until she got a little wet at the sight of a lamplit Clint Barrows in that cowboy hat, snug T-shirt and jeans.

Wonderful, faded, leg-hugging jeans....

"I saw you go out of the hotel by yourself," he said. "It's not exactly a concrete jungle out here, but it's dark."

He'd taken off his hat, the illumination making his hair look golden and so thick that it conjured naughty thoughts about that night all those years ago. Hot, dizzy, breath-stealing thoughts. Her mind went even further, and she pictured him kissing his way down her neck, her chest…lower, until he made his way across her stomach and then…

Her pulse was thudding in all the places she'd just pictured, as if his mouth was actually on her, driving her wild.

"Why're you really out here?" she asked, cooling herself off, making a show of corralling her luggage—which she did quite easily all on her own. A girl never traveled with more than she could handle.

As she headed back to the hotel, pulling her suitcase behind her, she walked closer to him. He was leaning back against what had to be his truck—a comfortable, beat-up blue Dodge—and he'd rested his hat on top of the cab, his thumbs hooked into his belt loops.

"I'm going to tell you my side of the story," he said. "Maybe not out here, maybe not at the kegger tomorrow, but you'll know it before the weekend comes to a close. And you'll know how much I regret what happened."

The soft rumble of her suitcase wheels went silent as she stopped just past him. "How could you regret it? You're the one who came off looking like a stud. I came off looking like something…rented."

She hadn't meant to say that much, but it'd come out, anyway.

His voice was low and, again, seemingly genuine. "I'm truly sorry about that, Margot."

She didn't like the way he said her name. Or, more to the point, she *did* like it. Way too much.

She turned to him, chin a notch higher than usual. "So what do you want to tell me? That Jay Halverson was behind all the camera stuff back in college? Because I've heard it all from Riley over the years."

"And you didn't believe him."

She only shrugged. She didn't owe him the truth.

Had she started to enjoy thinking he was the bad guy? Did it give her some kind of excuse to stay away?

His peace-offering grin stroked over her, and her heart lost a beat.

She girded herself. "Next thing you know, you'll be telling me that Jay posted that video last night."

"He did."

Okay, then. Mystery solved. "I guess that settles the score."

She started to leave.

"Not so fast." He'd lowered his voice to a sexy timbre, making her wonder why the hell she had her sights set on Brad, who was already in his room.

But she knew the answer. Brad was a known quantity, and maybe she needed someone safe this weekend, even as she imagined him part of some big adventure with her basket. Mild-mannered Brad had never broken her trust or given grist to the gossip mill with a video.

It'd bothered her more that her privacy had been violated, and especially that she'd been filmed with the playboy who'd had every other girl except her, it seemed.

Before she knew it, Clint had reached out, gently taking hold of her sweater, near the bottom. It gaped away from her body, the air like a caress, tickling her belly.

No, make that tickling her *everywhere,* especially in the last place she wanted Clint Barrows to be.

But she ached there, too, between her legs. Ached so badly.

He must've sensed that, because he tugged her closer. As the night breathed under the cashmere, she let go of her suitcase and stumbled toward him, close enough to smell the hay and clover on his clothing and skin.

The pure masculinity of him—the clean scent, the knowledge that there was muscle under his own shirt, so close, just a touch away—spiked desire through her.

"I'm going to make it all up to you," he said. "That's why I'm here."

She swallowed at his bold comment. A melting, lazy pull of sensation stretched in her, creating friction until there were sparks flaring in her stomach.

"You can't make up for what's been done," she said breathlessly.

He laughed, soft and low. "Sure I can. And in eighty ways, too."

Great—he must've overheard what the tag would be on her auction offering.

She grabbed his hand and tried to pull it away from her sweater. "That basket's not for you."

She realized her mistake right away, because beneath her palm and fingers, his skin was well worked, manly, strong. The feel of it fired a need through her that she hadn't realized was there, and it made her go even wetter for him.

"So you're saving yourself for another man," he said, twining his fingers through hers.

Oh, God, even such a simple connection sent the adrenaline racing through her, awakening her completely.

"Margot," he said softly. "You're being real difficult about this when it should be so easy."

But it wasn't. Not even close. Giving in to Clint Barrows was unthinkable at a reunion where everyone was just waiting for him to finally nail the one girl who'd slipped through his fingers.

Still, when he slid his other hand to her hip, massaging it with his thumb, she almost gave in.

She'd had too much to drink, she told herself. And she'd been lonely for the first time in her life because she was facing things she'd never faced before. All of that added up to a vulnerable Margot, and when he moved his hand to her backside, cupping her derriere, she sucked in a harsh breath.

"Just hear me out," he said.

Yes. It was on the tip of her tongue. It was screaming in her head, pulling her toward him even as she tried to stay away.

But it wasn't going to happen, because she still had a little something called pride.

"I've listened enough," she said.

She stepped away and grabbed her suitcase handle again, the wheels reverberating over the blacktop just as loudly as an unexpected, almost overwhelming hunger rumbled through her.

BY THE NEXT morning, Margot hadn't heard from Brad, and she told herself that it was still early—they had plenty of time before the auction.

And it wasn't as if she was depending on him for *the* best good time ever, anyway. She'd had pretty decent fun last night after she'd unpacked her suitcase, then met Leigh and Dani again in the café, where they'd caught up with other sisters who had offered solace about the video. That hadn't surprised Margot, because everyone but the biggest prudes had backed her up years ago when the first one had gone public.

Naturally, Margot had done her best to avoid the questions about future books and how well her sales were doing, all the while wondering if the concierge had gotten ahold of Brad yet with the "this is what my basket looks like" note and its less-than-subtle invitation to bid on it.

But there'd been some moments last night—a lot of them, actually—when she'd found her mind on someone else.

The cowboy with the cocky grin.

The man who'd used his sexy voice in the parking lot as if he were fully confident she was going to succumb to his supposedly irresistible charm.

Right.

She rolled out of bed, the digital clock on the nightstand blazing 9:00 a.m. in the dim room, darkened by the pulled heavy curtains. And when she glanced at the phone, the message light was dark, too, staring back at her blankly.

No calls.

But dammit all if she was going to bug the concierge by asking him if he'd even delivered the note to Brad.

Jeez, now she was wondering if it'd been such a good idea in the first place....

At least Leigh had told her last night that her note was a perfect prologue to her basket. Very old-school. And, hey, what guy wouldn't be interested in that kind of message?

Margot cracked the curtains, squinting at the sunlight. She smiled when she saw the wide tomato fields and the pine trees lining the nearby open road.

Unfortunately, her gaze then went to the parking lot, where she saw Clint Barrows's faded blue Dodge truck lounging next to her little Prius.

Why did it seem as if even his pickup was ready to devour her car?

Rubbing her arms, she wandered to the bathroom, turning on the shower, stripping off her long nightshirt. The second the heated mist whispered over her skin, she tightened with goose bumps, imagining that she heard a voice, soft and low, whispering quiet apologies to her.

Clint Barrows's apologies.

Just hear me out, he'd said last night in the parking lot, when she'd known he meant so much more.

She stepped into the shower, hoping the water would wash her into a sane place. But as it sluiced over her, she imagined his hand on her hip, just like last night when he'd been bold enough to touch her.

Yet, now, there were no clothes between them, and as she closed her eyes, the uninterrupted flutter of water against her became his fingers, and she felt them ease to her belly, a fleeting butterfly touch.

You're being real difficult about this when it should be so easy....

She leaned forward, bracing her hands against the tile wall. The water gently ran down her body, slipping over her thighs, in between her legs.

Wantonly, she opened them a little, loving the sensation as it skimmed over her clit.

The water became his fingers again, finding just the right spot, her breath quickening right along with her heartbeat.

You used to be a risk taker, she heard him tell her, as if they were talking again. The butterfly wings on her body traveled inward, beating in her belly, electric and tickling, making her bite her lip.

So why're you set on safe, boring Brad?

Why not go for this new direction?

She took her hand from the wall, trailed it between her breasts, down her stomach to her pulsing center. Sliding her fingers through her cleft, she massaged herself, thinking of Clint.

At least, with Brad, they'd had a summer together. And when they'd returned to college, after the bloom had faded off their little affair, they had floated away from each other, going different ways.

It'd all been perfectly safe with Brad, just as it could be this weekend. No deception, no videos.

But, as she touched herself, the water caressing her, the mere thought of that unpredictability sent a jolt through her, making her breath catch.

Wet. Excited. And every time she circled her clit with her thumb, imagining that it was Clint touching her, her temperature rose. The heat pushed her up, up, tighter and tighter, until a tiny series of impending explosions quivered in her.

She fought the first one, pressing herself forward against the wall....

Then the second, as it rolled through her, shake by contained shake....

But the third—

She started to give in to it for the first time in months, slipping down the wall as blasts of sensation seized her, making her gasp just before she let go with one long, hard inhale...then...

As the water ran over her—just water now—she groaned, aching.

Still aching.

And hardly knowing just what it was anymore that she really wanted.

4

AFTER THE PREGAME party and the homecoming football match itself, the reunion moved to Main Street, to the back room of Dani's favorite hangout in Avila Grande.

Desperado's was one of those country joints that was marked by the smell of hops and fried food every time you walked through its swinging doors and hit the planked floor. On the walls above the bar were deer antlers, a buffalo head and a menu that showcased Rocky Mountain Oysters—a dish that Dani didn't have the stomach for once Leigh and Margot had told her that the name was actually a euphemism for bull-calf testicles.

Ah, yes, good old Desperado's, where the Valley's farm and ranch kids had hung out, where music had always been 100 percent country, the beer cheap and the food rugged and, as it turned out, disgusting.

But the moment Dani had strolled in with Riley tonight, greeted by the thud of hip-hop and the sight of undergrads doing everything but the two-step on the small dance floor, it was obvious things had changed.

"So it's come to this," Dani said as she and Riley left the main room and made their way through the slim lantern-lit corridor toward the back, where the auction was scheduled to start in an hour. "Desperado's is now pure evil."

"Evil?" Riley rested a hand on the back of her neck, cupping it. "Strong word, Dan."

"Okay, maybe not *evil,* then. It's just…" She motioned toward the dance floor and almost flinched at the loud music, which was making them raise their voices. "I miss how it used to be."

He guided her to the side of the corridor. No one else was there right now—they were early. And when he leaned back against the wall, putting his hands on her jeaned hips, pulling her to him, her heart jittered. But it was always that way when she looked into Riley's deep blue eyes.

"I don't like it, either," he said. "But things never stay the same. Not anywhere."

"I guess I'm just getting old and cranky." She'd also felt that way before the game, while walking around campus. Dressed in her old Cal-U sweatshirt against the fall chill in the air, she'd felt like a grandma next to all the students running around, their lives ahead of them as they dreamed of success. "Everything just seems so…corporate. Cal-U used to be small, homier. Now it's—"

"Trendier than hell. I noticed."

He bent forward, kissing her forehead, and they stayed like that for a few seconds, his breath stirring her hair, infiltrating her, just as it had ever since she'd glanced up one day on a sorority/fraternity reunion cruise five years ago that neither Leigh nor Margot had signed up for. That's when she'd seen Riley giving her that look—one she'd never noticed before. It was the look of a friend who had apparently been thinking some extremely more-than-buddies thoughts without her even knowing it until that moment.

It had changed her world, changed her mind.

But it hadn't changed either of *them*.

Or so she'd believed. It hadn't occurred to her that change was everywhere except in her until last night, when Margot and Leigh had sprung this auction on her.

She held on to Riley, her hands wrapped in the bottom of his long, untucked shirt, cocooned there. After last night, she'd started wondering just how people perceived her—had *always* perceived her.

Was she someone in need of rescuing? A pitiful dreamy princess who'd been defined all her life by one goal and one goal only?

To be the ultimate bridezilla?

Just…wow. And, the thing was, Dani feared that her friends were right. What had she done with herself all these years besides get a job as lead caterer for someone else's company? What true ambitions had she possessed?

She'd always looked up to Margot—and who hadn't? Margot led the pack, getting them into trouble while watching over them at the same time. Dani loved her friend's independence, her go-get-'em approach to life. And the same went for Leigh, who had overcome a tragic childhood filled with sadness after the accidental drowning of her sister. Leigh had also struggled with her weight when she was younger, but now she was as svelte as Margot and just as successful a businesswoman. And what was Dani?

Down the corridor, she heard a door close, and she caught a peek of Margot, dressed as stunningly as ever in what looked to be an Ann Taylor leather jacket, a pencil skirt and high boots as she made a beeline for the back room. She was carrying an iPad, probably to keep track of the baskets that had already been dropped off, and she didn't see Dani and Riley as she disappeared.

Riley's voice rumbled through his chest as he spoke. Dani could feel it while she pressed against him.

"Do you think Margot's pissed after what you told her at the game?" he asked.

"Not pissed. Disappointed, I'd say." After Dani and Riley had talked this whole auction thing over last night, they'd decided that Margot and Leigh could still hold the event—it just wouldn't be for their wedding. Instead, he had suggested a charity that fed the homeless in Avila Grande.

"She'll get over it," Riley said.

"I'm sure she's already knee-deep in the excitement of tonight." But, still, Dani *had* seen disappointment in both Margot's and Leigh's eyes this afternoon. They clearly hadn't believed her when she'd told them that it didn't matter *how* she and Riley got married—a small ceremony, an elopement. Whatever. She and Riley had been together for long enough that marriage was only a piece of paper to them.

Or maybe Dani had just been saying this so often that she believed it. And Riley, being Riley, hadn't pushed her on the subject too hard. He'd heard enough stories about the curveball her parents had thrown her just before she and Riley had gotten together. Married thirty-seven years, obviously just pretending to be happy, then *boom*.

Divorce. Because of a cheating dad.

As if knowing what had entered her thoughts again, Riley stroked her curls away from her face. Patient, wonderful Riley, who'd waited around long enough for her to finally start planning a wedding after the fallout from her mom and dad.

"Is Margot excited because she thinks Brad is going to bid on her basket?" he asked, knowing just how to change a subject.

Dani smiled up at him. "No doubt. It's strange, though, because never in a million years would I think that a woman of experience like Margot would be in to a garden-variety type like Brad these days."

"Clint's in to her."

"What? When did you find this out?"

"Last night. You went out with the girls, and I was asleep when you got back, and then we had breakfast with the others and the game…"

Little time for talking. Or much else. "Margot told me and Leigh that she had an 'incident' with Clint in the parking lot last night. She stiff-armed him, though. Doesn't trust him as far as she can throw him, even though he's told her that Jay was the culprit who posted the video."

"It doesn't matter to Margot, does it?"

"Nope. I think that, if she gives Clint the time of day, it'll be like she's surrendering or something. Like there's this battle of wills going on, and it started way back when she didn't want to be one of his many women."

"Until she *was*."

Dani gave him a light push. "Hey, they didn't have sex. She didn't give in to him at all."

They laughed. It was always so easy to do with each other.

Then Dani said, "Margot has this idea that she's going to re-create her golden summer with Brad or something."

"We'll see. He wasn't at the game, and I thought he said this morning during fishing that he would be."

"You think he's going to ditch the auction, then?"

Riley shrugged. "If he does that, he should've let Margot know. She sent him that note."

"And don't you dare let her know I told you. She'd kill me if she heard I was letting you in on everything."

"Hey—we're about to get married. People expect us to share."

The intimate comment made her shoulders tense ever so slightly. Just because people got married, it didn't guarantee that they'd be some eternal, single entity. Or maybe, for a time at the beginning, it *did* mean just that, and when things went wrong and you had to rip yourself away from your other, the wound would never heal.

She'd seen proof of it in her mom and dad, who still didn't speak to each other unless they had to.

Riley's arms tightened around her, and she locked gazes with him. Somewhere along the way, the wind had ruffled his dark hair enough so that he had bedhead, and it gave him a boyish look that nicked her heart. And his smile… It was sexy and youthful, both at the same time.

They wouldn't turn out the way her parents had. She told herself that every day.

"I've heard enough about Brad," she said softly, losing herself in his eyes as deeply as she had ever allowed herself to be lost.

Then she put her arms around him and hugged him even closer, shutting her eyes out of pure instinct so she wouldn't get *too* lost.

AN HOUR AND a half later, Clint reclined in a chair at the rear of the back room in Desperado's, his hat tipped back on his head, his boots propped on the table in front of him. He'd stayed distant from the crowd as they joked and jested and gathered near the front, where the baskets were set out in an anonymous parade of color and ruffles.

But it was Margot who had his full attention. Margot Walker, with her fancy, big-city, spike-heeled boots, short straight brown skirt and creamy top that clung to her curves.

And, boy, had he felt a few of those curves last night when he'd impulsively met her in the parking lot, intending to help with her luggage, only to decide on the turn of a dime to try a little bit of something else.

Maybe he'd been too aggressive though, because, once again, he'd been shot down in flames.

Clint grinned to himself. Yep, he'd been put in his place, but there'd been one moment—a hesitation, a heartbeat—when he'd seen something in her eyes.

Something that told him she was wondering what it'd be like with him. Something that hinted she enjoyed being touched the way he was touching her.

And that was all Clint had needed to come here tonight, to this basket auction.

The president of his pledge class, Walt Tolliver, who'd been on the student body and had gone on to run successfully for his local town council, had volunteered to lead the charity auction since Margot and Leigh were the ones who'd turned tonight into a charity event.

Margot stood by, handing out the baskets as the bidders won them. By now, they'd gotten to the last few. And, wouldn't you know it, hers hadn't come up for auction just yet.

But Clint could wait.

He'd been setting aside "fun money" for years, never using it for vacations or the like. On the interest alone, he could afford to spend a pretty penny tonight, especially because he'd also been saving for possible legal fees with his brothers.

But this was as much fun as any money could buy. He also wanted to make this auction a major success for Margot.

And the time was getting near.

Margot picked up a "basket" that was actually a large pot with the word "honey" painted on the outside, and she set it on the podium where Walt waited.

"Who's looking for a taste of honey?" he asked, weaving the title of the basket into his question, just as he'd been doing all night.

Clint's fraternity brothers laughed and catcalled about honey-this and honey-that, but he refrained. The basket with the gold and silver stars would come up soon enough, and as Margot swept another surreptitious glance around the room, Clint wondered if she had put off bringing her basket up for auction because her dear Brad was MIA.

Looked as if she had no idea that ol' Bradley Harrington had been called home on business. Wasn't that a bummer?

"Bidding starts at a hundred bucks," Walt said, looking for takers.

"*Two* hundred," shouted Ed Kendrick. "I could use some sweetening."

Before everyone stopped laughing, another brother, Mark Heinbeck, yelled, "Three hundred."

As the bidding continued, Dani and Riley sat down at Clint's table. The two of them got cozy in their chairs, leaning back and surveying the controlled chaos. Riley was holding a red, white and blue basket with curly streamers, which Dani had put together at the last minute. He'd won it, no problem, because of course no one would dare step on Riley's toes.

"Just think," Clint said, leaning toward Riley so his voice wouldn't carry over Walt's calls. "You could've had some real cash thrown at that wedding of yours tonight. They're raking it in."

"I'm glad it's going where it's going," Riley said, exchanging a grin with Dani.

Clint noticed a shadow in Dani's eyes, but then something happened at the front of the room that pulled his focus there.

A woman had stepped forward to bid on the honey basket, and Clint recognized her as Beth Dahrling, a sorority sister who was a couple years older than he was. She was wearing a conservative skirt set, her long dark hair held back by an expensive-looking shell barrette.

"Five thousand," she said smoothly.

Everyone in the room froze, even Clint. Then someone whispered to another person, and a gossipy hum filled the place.

Up in front, Margot was staring wide-eyed at Leigh, who was sedately lounging in her chair in a corner, a cowboy-booted foot propped over her knee. The only thing besides Margot's expression that confirmed this basket was Leigh's was the too-cool way she didn't move a muscle.

The room went quiet as everyone else glanced at Leigh, too. Hell, nobody had expected a woman to bid on another woman's basket, and Clint wasn't sure Leigh swung that way.

Dani shifted in her chair, and Riley stifled a grin just before his fiancée smacked his leg.

Walt cleared his throat. "Five thousand going once?" he asked, obviously testing Leigh.

She smiled, then laughed, making a bring-it-on motion with her hands.

Margot smiled at her, then at Beth Dahrling, who gave Leigh a little friendly wave, then said, "I'm here for someone else, Leigh. Don't panic."

A buzz rose in the room as people started to ask just what Beth was up to. But the woman remained silent, shrugging and calmly grinning.

Riley leaned toward Clint. "Glad I didn't put the kibosh on this auction, after all."

President Walt was calling for order, and when he got a semblance of it, he yelled, "Is there anyone here who can beat five thou? It's for charity."

When he didn't get any takers, he held up his gavel. "Okay. Going once…twice…" *Bang.* "Sold!"

The applause was louder than usual as Margot took the basket to Beth, and Leigh, with her typical sense of humor, stood and went to her fellow sorority sister, linking arms with her and walking out of the room with an exaggerated sashay of her Wrangler-clad rump.

"Nothing's gonna top that," Riley muttered as the noise died down and Margot picked up another basket.

I can think of at least eighty things that very well could, Clint thought, barely keeping track of the last few auction items before they finally came to Margot's offering.

Almost time…

Just before Margot went to the table, slowly picking up her basket, Clint noticed Leigh slipping into the room and leaning against a wall, a furrow to her brow as she stood alone, without Beth.

President Walt rubbed his hands together. "Wonder whose *this* could be...."

Every guy who hadn't won a basket tonight hooted and whistled; it was obvious that Margot hadn't walked out of the room with anyone yet, and the basket had to be hers. She gave a sassy, narrowed glance to the room in general, but Clint could tell that she was indulging in one last scan for Brad.

For a moment, Clint swore that Walt was about to make a joke about the video, but then he only grinned. Clint nodded slightly to him.

"Let's start with a hundred for what promises to be a very exotic offering," Walt said. "Around the Girl in—"

Margot cut him off. "It's a travel basket. That's all."

Clint laughed. She was playing down the spicy title, wasn't she? Those cards in the basket would be worded so vaguely that she could give the winner a hot date or a cool one, depending on whoever won.

He'd take his chances.

Since he didn't want to seem too eager, he waited out the initial bidders. It was only when he snagged Margot's gaze as she surveyed the room again that he finally rose to his feet, lethargically sweeping off his hat.

"Six hundred," he said with great relish as he met Margot's gaze.

There was a sizzling connection between them as she glared right back.

He thought he heard a few *oohs* in the room. If they couldn't talk about the video, they'd certainly *ooh* about it.

One of the sorority sisters said, "Don't get slapped this time, Clint," and that caused somewhat of a minor kerfuffle. It also caused Margot's laserlike glare to intensify.

"I bid seven hundred," she said.

That got a rise out of the room. And, truth be told, it did the same to Clint, too.

Riley punched Clint's side and gave him a challenging look. *Yeah, don't get slapped.*

Clint propped his booted foot on his chair and leaned his elbow on his thigh. He could do this all night.

"Eight hundred," he said.

"Nine," she shot back.

Walt laughed right along with everyone else before saying, "Hate to tell you, Margot, but you can't bid. It's against the rules."

"Hey," she said, clutching her basket to her. "I organized this auction."

"Oooh," went the crowd again.

But then Leigh drawled from her side of the room. "You're not the only one who put this thing together, Marg, and I say you're breaking the rules."

A bigger *"Oooh."*

If looks could kill, Leigh would be in a million pieces. It was pretty obvious that the friendly one-upmanship between her and Margot hadn't died since college had ended, but Leigh obviously thought this whole thing was hilarious.

Margot? Not so much.

"I'll tell you what," Clint said, after holding up his hand for silence. "Let's just make it an even thousand and call it a night. There're people who have baskets to open."

"But—" Margot said.

Walt hit the gavel on the podium before Margot could get too far, and Riley stood, pushing Clint forward. His brothers patted him on the back as he made his way to the front, his gaze never leaving Margot's.

A thousand bucks was going to put a real dent in his fun money for the year, but he didn't have any vacations planned.

Except for the ones Margot's basket had arranged.

He planted himself in front of her, nodding at the basket that she was hugging for the life of her, just as Walt yelled, "Sold!"

But from the looks of his date, Clint was pretty sure that she was anything but.

5

EARLY SUNDAY AFTERNOONS were usually Margot's favorite. They were a time for sleeping in, then lounging on the balcony of her condo with a cup of tea while taking in the view of the fruit trees and bricked walkways that decorated her complex. They were full of sunny moments reading the paper, savoring the scones she liked to pick up at the local bakery the night before.

But *this* Sunday?

Was the polar opposite. And Dani seemed to sense it, too, as she took a seat across from Margot at the hotel's café, where only a few other customers were talking quietly over late breakfasts.

Luckily, none of them had been at the auction last night, so Margot had been enjoying a little peace while waiting for both Leigh and Dani before they wiled away the hours before the final event—a formal dinner at the hotel.

"Morning, sunshine," Dani said, plopping into her seat with an impish grin. She looked just as fresh as a rose, her red curls pulled back into a ponytail and a white blouse tied at the waist. A high flush colored her smooth, pale cheeks.

Nice to know that *someone* in the hotel had enjoyed a good night. "Peppy, aren't you?"

"I had a great time last night. Why shouldn't I be full of smiles when I was so highly entertained? If you hadn't taken off like a shot after the auction—and if you'd returned my calls—we could've had a good laugh about things over drinks."

"I texted you back." Margot had wanted to be by herself, where she couldn't see everyone's amusement as the reunion continued.

Didn't Dani get it? Clint Barrows had been instrumental in embarrassing her publicly once before and here he was again, bidding on her basket, making sure everyone knew that he was still the fraternity stud and that being slapped back in college wasn't going to stop him.

The waiter interrupted, and Dani asked for orange juice and fried eggs. Margot, who already had her Earl Grey tea, ordered a fruit bowl. Leigh had asked her to get black-as-night coffee and waffles topped with lots of fresh strawberries.

After the server had left, Margot took up where their conversation stopped. "So last night tickled your funny bone."

"I wouldn't put it that way."

"Good. Because there wasn't much that was funny about it."

"Margot." Dani smiled gently. "It's not every night that someone pays a thousand smackaroos for one of my best friends. Can't you see what a compliment that was? As far as I'm concerned, Clint was showing that

he values you. It would've been more embarrassing if
your basket had gone for peanuts."

Right. A thousand-dollar bid. Margot didn't want
to even consider what kind of indecent proposals Clint
Barrows was no doubt thinking he would discover inside her basket.

Perv.

"It wasn't a compliment," Margot said, cupping both
hands around her mug. "Clint just wanted to show everyone that he's out to close the deal on that video."

"But that was years ago." Dani cleared her throat as
the waiter brought her juice. An elderly couple passed
their table, and she lowered her voice. "Riley says that
Clint doesn't have anything up his sleeve."

"Fraternity brothers. They look out for each other…
unless they're Jay Halverson."

"Who got blackballed, by the way. And Riley
wouldn't lie to me about Clint."

Dani just sat there for a moment, long enough so
that Margot stopped fiddling with her mug and settled
back into her seat.

"He says Clint's changed, and he's got some very real
adult problems to deal with now. For one thing, his two
brothers are trying to force him into doing business on
his ranch their way."

A surprising pang hit Margot. Maybe it was because
she'd always had a soft spot for underdogs. But…Clint?
She'd never seen such an arrogant one, so she doubted
her instincts.

"How can his brothers do that if it's not their ranch?"
she asked.

A small smile lit Dani's face. She obviously thought
Margot was interested or something.

"Clint's father left him the majority percentage of

the ranch after he passed away, but they've been hinting that, since they own a part of it, they might get legal about the way the ranch is being run." Dani shrugged. "But I don't do business, so what do I know?"

Margot hated when Dani got like this—lacking in confidence. "You could've had your own business, Dan. Still could."

Dani didn't say anything, but she had a faraway look in her eyes.... A hint of something that Margot had never seen there before, as if she was really thinking about what Margot had said for the first time since they'd known each other.

But it disappeared when Leigh arrived, dressed in a fancy, silver-threaded cowgirl shirt that nipped in at the waist, plus jeans and a pair of hand-worked boots. She'd fixed her blond hair into a low braid that hung down her back.

She sat, resting a booted ankle on her knee, stretching her arms as if she'd just rolled out of bed.

"Finally," Margot said, signaling to the waiter to bring Leigh's coffee. "Someone who can take the heat off me about last night."

"Oh, goody," Leigh said, putting her hands behind her head and closing her eyes. "We have to launch into *this* first thing."

Dani brightened up. "No matter how many drinks we plied you with last night, we couldn't get the truth out of you about your bidder."

"And why should I start pouring out my soul this morning?" Leigh asked, accepting a mug from the waiter and blowing on her steaming coffee.

As Margot and Dani darted expectant looks at her, Leigh finally rolled her eyes in surrender.

"There's nothing to report, girls. I don't know any

more information about who won my basket than I did twelve hours ago."

"Nothing?" Margot asked.

"Nothing. Beth Dahrling said she'd been instructed not to tell me much—just that a secret admirer had asked her to represent him at the auction. Apparently, he's out of town on business for a while, and that's why he sent a representative."

"Aren't you wary of the situation?" Dani asked, but the rush of excitement in her voice made her a liar.

Margot waggled her eyebrows. "So he's got to be one of the brothers. I'm going to get on the computer and do some research, narrow it down, come up with an answer."

"I already did a search," Dani said. "I haven't come up with any candidates who can afford to spend five thou on a basket."

Leigh shrugged. "Don't bother trying anymore."

"Is there anyone you're hoping it is?" Margot asked.

She anticipated what came next: Leigh getting that "who cares?" posture, one arm resting on the back of her chair, the rest of her body just as languid.

"You all know me," she drawled. "Chubby girls don't get a lot of action in college, so I didn't bother with crushes. I didn't pay much attention to the brothers in that way, and I can't believe any of them paid much mind to me."

She was half-right. Leigh had been just as focused as Margot on her studies, doing a lot of side projects like creating campus cookbooks and working on the Cal-U Rodeo Days as one of the student board members each year. But now, after the weight loss and a whole lot of career success, things had to be different for Leigh.

Right?

Margot surveyed her for a second, and Leigh squirmed in her chair.

"Just say it," she muttered.

"Well, clearly someone paid attention to you," Margot said.

"Or," Leigh shot back, "they saw my show on TV and they suddenly got interested. Let's not make this into some epic love story."

"I don't know." Margot leaned back again. "It's all so very mysterious and hot. A secret admirer for our Lee-Lee."

She chuffed. "Don't you sit there all smug, just like you're not caught up in as much fallout from the auction."

Dani interrupted. "You two brought it on yourselves."

Margot pointed at her. "And who's the smug one now?"

"I'm not the girl who's going to be going eighty ways to Ha-cha-cha-ville with my college enemy," Dani said. "So I do feel pretty smug about my stress-free fiancé at the moment."

Margot made a point of calmly refreshing her tea with the hot water pot. "I'm not going anywhere with Clint Barrows."

Leigh stopped drinking her coffee. "Maybe you need a refresher course on what happened last night."

Ha-ha. "I'm going to get out of this. Just watch me."

Dani laughed. "How's that?"

"I'll just give him back his money."

Both of her friends sighed, but not before Margot caught them glancing at each other.

"What?" she asked.

Leigh punched her in the arm, kind of hard, too, and Margot pressed a hand to her skin.

"Ouch," she said. Cowgirl Leigh had always been strong.

"If I'm going through with this basket thing," she said, "you'd better do it, too."

"Or what?"

"Or you'll regret it."

"Why? Because you'll call me a chicken for the rest of my life?"

"No," Leigh said. "Because you'll be calling yourself a chicken. I know you, Margot—when you were sparring with Clint at that auction, you lit up. You liked it."

"I was pissed that he would come after me like he did."

"You were excited."

Margot opened her mouth to retort, but she didn't have anything to counter.

Because Leigh was 100 percent on target. Margot *had* been excited, and she'd been praying for all she was worth that no one would notice.

Especially him.

But it wasn't as if she was going to let Leigh know that she'd scored a direct hit. Hell, no.

She reached down to her Gucci tote bag and pulled out her iPad, turning it on and changing the subject so thoroughly that both Dani and Leigh laughed under their breaths.

"I'm not going to waste my time talking about him," Margot said, accessing a file on the screen. "Not when I spent most of the night being gainfully occupied."

She didn't add that she hadn't been able to get to sleep, anyway. Not with Clint Barrows on her mind... and under her skin.

When she showed Dani the wedding-dress pictures that she'd stored in an e-file, her friend went quiet, just as she had the other day after the news about the auction.

"I have a friend," Margot said, treading lightly now, wondering if Dani would be offended by her wedding-planning initiative once again. "She designs gowns, and she doesn't cost an arm and a leg because I'm sure I can work a deal with her. I thought you might want to take a peek at her designs."

Dani didn't take the iPad. "You know someone who offers discounted wedding venues, too? And cakes? How about massage oils and sex toys, Margot?"

She laughed a little, and Margot took the iPad back. Yep, she'd overstepped, just as she and Leigh had done when they'd set up the auction without Dani's knowledge in the first place.

As if she realized that she'd caused Margot discomfort, Dani smiled that sunny smile and held out her hand.

"Let's see what you've got," she said.

As Margot handed over the computer, she caught Leigh's eye. She winked at her, and Margot returned the gesture.

Wedding dress viewing soon turned into an online search for venues as they ate breakfast, and soon the late-morning crowd had turned into an early-lunch one.

They paid up, then exited the café, catching an elevator to their rooms.

"See you at the dinner tonight?" Leigh asked as the panel dinged at Margot's floor.

The door opened, and over her shoulder, she said, "Sure. I'll be the one hiding in the corner."

"As if," Dani said, before the doors closed on her and Leigh.

Margot smiled while she walked down the hall toward her room. Yeah, they all knew damned well that she wouldn't be hiding from anyone, especially Clint. After Margot returned his money, she was planning to dance the night away and show him just who had come out on top in this little power game they were playing.

She rounded a corner, so intent on finding her key card in her tote bag that she didn't notice that someone was waiting for her.

When that someone took her by the waist and scooped her into the ice-machine alcove, her breath was already halfway out of her lungs.

And when that someone turned out to be Clint Barrows grinning down at her, his light blue eyes full of amusement, Margot lost her breath—and her will—altogether.

CLINT'S HAND RESTED on her waist while the other tipped up his cowboy hat.

"You sure took your sweet time at breakfast," he said. "I couldn't help seeing you and the girls in that café and wondering just when you'd be done."

Even though he had her cornered near the ice machine, a pulsating wisp of space between their bodies, she didn't take the escape route.

But maybe that was only because she couldn't resist the opportunity to sass him.

"Just to be clear," she said tightly, "I was planning on writing you a check for every cent you spent on that basket."

"A refund?" He ran his gaze over the dark, long layers of her hair, then up to her face, with those startling pale eyes fringed with sweeping lashes, those red lips...

The words almost snagged in his throat. "I'm not interested in getting my money back."

Her pupils had gone wide, as if, with every look he smoothed over her, she was forgetting how much she couldn't stand him. His gut tightened with heat and yearning.

That night, so long ago... Their kisses...

No, he didn't want a refund. He wanted a replay.

And this time he wanted it all to turn out right, without her burning rubber after she thought he'd humiliated her.

"What makes you think you run the show here?" she asked, her voice softer now. "What makes you think you have any sort of choice about what I do?"

"Darlin'," he said, "letting me have your basket could be the best choice you've ever made."

He grinned down at her and, for an expanding second, he thought she might close her eyes, invite him to kiss her, tell him that bygones were bygones and...

What?

It wouldn't go beyond that, but at least he'd go home happy before getting real unhappy with his brothers again.

Before being isolated from what was left of his family.

But she seemed to snap out of it, nudging away from him, taking off just as quickly as she had done all those years ago, except without the slap and the door slamming.

"Margot," he said, following her out of the small room and into the hallway.

"Don't 'Margot' me when we've got nothing to 'Margot' about. I forgot my checkbook in my room, but I'm going to write you the fastest check I've ever written in my life."

His steps were twice the length of hers, and in no time, he'd come to the front of his own room, deftly slipping his key card into the reader, then opening his door.

She started to pass him, then paused, obviously unable to stop herself from peering inside.

And why not, when he'd raided that fancy-schmancy store in the downtown village of Avila Grande bright and early, just to create his own version of a basket?

Step one, win her over.

Step two, win *her*.

He'd been waiting for Margot to finish breakfast to set his intentions into motion. And, after slipping one of the desk clerks a hefty tip, he'd even made sure that he transferred to a room on her floor.

He opened the door a little wider, so she could get a better view of the bamboo stand he'd set up near the entrance. The faux candle in it cast a dim, sultry light over the sheer scarves he'd draped over the small dressing screen he'd found in the same shop.

"What the hell is this?" she asked.

He only shrugged. Her question had an edge, but Clint knew an intrigued woman when he heard one, and he stepped aside to let the adventuress see more.

She was the woman who'd taken off to Europe after college to "experience life," according to her bio in the back of the books he'd also purchased today. The woman who'd pushed her travels further when she'd gone on to write about sexy swims in hidden pools on the paradise roads of Maui and about the most enticing foods to be found in exotic places like Shanghai.

The smart, seductive woman he'd seen in her that

night, one who had taken her fantasies and made them realities.

He left the door open as she crossed his threshold and looked around at the dressing screen, then the items he'd arranged near it.

A tray full of truffles and chocolate-drizzled croissants from the bakery downtown.

A basket of bubble bath, lotion and sinuously carved soaps.

A beautiful white slip of a negligee that was as innocent as it was suggestive.

She slid him a look out of the corner of her eye. "Did you go to The Boudoir?"

"I made a stop." The boutique had been around since their college days, a Cal-U institution. "But I also hit a few other places."

"Why?"

"Because I went through all those slips of paper you have in that basket." He pulled one of the scenarios from his back pocket and read it. "'The Grand Palace in Thailand, home of a king.' I couldn't get too fancy at such short notice, though I figured you'd like the truffles at the very least."

Did she look…touched?

But he wasn't sure, because her expression went back to normal—amused, cool. Margot.

He said, "You really did word those scenarios carefully, didn't you?"

She narrowed her gaze at him, but she didn't go anywhere. He took that as a good sign and allowed the door to ease shut behind him. The soft click of the lock was the only sound besides the thud of his heartbeat.

Any minute now, she was going to tell him to go to hell.

Any minute now, he would feel just as confused as he'd been that night when she'd acted as if their kisses hadn't affected her as much as they had him. If she'd been as turned inside out as he was, she would've believed him about Jay and the camera. Or at least she would've come back to him after accepting his explanations.

But Margot surprised him, reaching out to touch one of the scarves hanging from the dressing screen.

Could keeping her in this room really be that easy?

"You went to a lot of work," she said.

"I take my investments seriously."

Holding his breath, he stepped toward her, daring to touch her hair.

Soft. Just as silky as one of those scarves. His blood screamed through him.

As he skimmed his hand downward, over her shoulder blade, he heard her inhale.

Was she going to run?

Or would she stay and let him make every fantasy he'd had over the past ten years come true?

EVEN WITH THE silk of her shirt as a barrier between his fingers and her skin, Margot could feel the heat of him seeping into her, flowing downward, flooding her with jagged pinpoints of need.

Her pride told her to get out of there, but her body…

Her body wasn't moving, just like the other night when he'd waylaid her in the parking lot, touching her, flirting with her until she'd almost melted into his arms.

She was pounding all over, craving him in a way that only a memory could bring on—a memory of that night the camera had recorded them.

Part of her wanted to show him that he would never

have her. Show him that she wasn't going to lose this contest of wills between them.

The other part of her knew it was a bad, bad idea to be here at all, because he was Clint Barrows, bane of her existence.

But it was another, steamier part that was winning yet again. Hands down.

Shivers spilled through her as his fingertips traced down her back, over her spine. Shivers that speared her, tingling, destroying every resisting thought.

His voice was low, hot.

"Your basket promised eighty ways around a girl," he said, his breath stirring the hair by her ear. "But I'll bet I could find eighty other ways all on my own, without your help."

He skimmed his fingertips to the base of her spine, slipped under her blouse, touched her with the lightest of strokes.

She flinched at the bare contact.

"Seems I've found number one," he said.

God, he sounded so arrogant. And why shouldn't he be when he was reducing her to a pool of thick honey and making her stay when she knew she should go?

He found the zipper at the back of her suede skirt, and when he started to pull it down, the sound ripped through her.

Stay? Go?

Her mind was a mess, reeling with desire.

As he tucked a finger between her and the skirt, skimming just over the line of her panties, she bit her lip, keeping herself from responding. Even so, a little moan escaped her.

"Way number two," he said.

He left her zipper partly open, resting his other hand

on her hip, then tugging lightly at the waistline. Air hushed against her exposed skin, and she turned her face away from him.

It'd be a good time to tell him to stop.

A real good time.

When he coaxed a finger into her skirt, exploring her hipbone, then wandering over to whisk over her belly, her stomach muscles jumped, and she leaned forward, one hand seeking the low dresser for balance.

"Three," he said.

As he ran that finger down toward her panty line, she canted forward a bit more, both hands on the dresser now, her breath sharp, hard to come by.

He coasted his finger beneath the front elastic of her panties, back and forth, stirring her up until she was stiff and achy and oh-so drenched.

Four, she thought.

He didn't have to count anymore as he went lower, more aggressive now, sliding that finger between her folds, making her take a step forward and gasp, then part her legs for him.

What was she doing?

It didn't matter, because she'd already given him all the permission he needed to do whatever it was he'd planned. And she didn't care.

Didn't care one damned bit now.

As he caressed her, up, down, around her clit, she didn't try to stay cool with him anymore. A moan escaped her, and she pressed back against him, feeling his erection.

He cupped a breast with his other hand, his mouth at her ear. "You were already wet for me, Margot."

She ignored the taunt, moving with every motion he made, instead.

Hadn't she imagined something like this in the shower yesterday? His hands, his fingers, then his mouth, all over her, building up a fire in her, pressure, pushing down, up, out, all over the place until—

He thrust two fingers up and into her, and she cried out, mostly because his thumb was working her clit with masterful care, just as if he'd already gone eighty times around her and wasn't about to stop there.

In, out… She wasn't going to last much longer, not with this need to explode. Not with the stiffness of his cock pressed against the back of her.

She wanted him to rip off her skirt, her panties, then pound all the way into her…

Bringing her higher…

Pushing her faster, harder—

An orgasm ripped through her with such force that she sucked in a breath that nearly cut her in two. Once. Then again. And he kept massaging her clit until she couldn't stand anymore and she was suddenly on the floor, boneless, clutching at the dresser. He'd come down to the ground with her, his hand still in her panties as if he owned that part of her.

Now she really couldn't move. Too weak. Too…

She had to admit it. She'd never reacted this way with any man in any country, whether he was a seductive stranger she'd built up in her mind to *ooo-la-la* levels or if he was a short-term fling she'd lost interest in after they'd gotten what they'd needed from each other.

As he pulled out of her, she almost told him not to. He felt too right in her, and she wondered just how right more of him than his fingers would feel. But she also wondered what the college girl who had been humiliated by a joke—and, truthfully, crushed by the realization that Clint really was just a Casanova—would've thought if she could see adult Margot now.

She was slumped back against him, and when she realized that his arm was cradled over her—his possessive, muscled arm—a shock of warmth tumbled through her.

It felt like…affection. But that was impossible when she and Clint Barrows didn't know each other from Eve and Adam.

He was straightening her skirt, tugging it to cover her modestly, and that struck her, too. It struck her so hard that she straightened up and got to her knees, pushing his arm away from her as she took up the job of fixing her own clothes.

"Well," she said. "I guess you got a good return on your investment."

He didn't answer, and without thinking, she peered over her shoulder to see why.

His knees were up, his arms resting on them. Somewhere along the way, his cowboy hat had fallen off, and his golden hair was mussed.

Her heart jerked in her chest, the dumb thing.

"Believe it or not," he said, "I wanted to take this step by step with you."

"Take what?"

He laughed. "Whatever was going to happen with us."

Now she laughed, but it wasn't out of gaiety. "You're sure full of yourself, aren't you? Bringing me in here and thinking…"

"That something *would* happen?" He glanced at her waistline, where her blouse was still untucked. "Call me crazy."

She didn't know whether to hate him or hop on him.

Truthfully, though, she knew it wasn't Clint she hated—it was the fact that she'd given in without much of a fight, and she wanted to do a lot more of it, too.

Clint sighed, running a hand through his hair roughly. "Margot, if you're thinking that you're going to come out of this room looking like a fool because you got together with me, don't. What happened in the past is water under the bridge."

"Not when everyone was served up a memory the other night, after that video rose from the dead." She had already gotten to her feet.

His chest constricted. "No one cares. Let it go."

"Why? Why is it so important?"

He raised both hands, then let them fall back down. "I told you—I feel bad for everything that happened."

He said it as if there was more.

But she didn't want to press him. Once she got back home, real life would take over. No more baskets, no more of the animating spark that Clint seemed to bring to her life.

A blush roared up to her face at the realization that he was more than just an enemy. Wait until everyone heard about *this*. Wait until they were all laughing over their beers, acting like college kids again, gossiping about how Clint Barrows had finally closed the deal.

He seemed to read her thoughts. "They wouldn't have to know."

She stared at him as his meaning sank in. She'd told him that once, before kissing him on his college couch.

He grinned that Romeo grin. "If you want to show me the rest of what's in that basket tonight—and just tonight—no one would ever be the wiser. And I mean that."

Her sense of adventure flared up, but there was more to it than that.

Her body wouldn't forget what he had done to it, and she was already hungering for more. Damn her crazy libido, she was already jonesing for something that had been absolutely unthinkable just a night before, and she didn't know how it'd happened or even when she'd made the choice for it to happen.

Slowly, she tucked in her blouse. And, in spite of everything, when she was done, she decided to tell Clint Barrows just what he could do with that basket.

6

DAMN, MARGOT WAS a tease.

After their encounter, Clint had retreated to familiar ground, going with Riley to the Phi Rho Mu house just off the Cal-U campus. The fall leaves colored the trees and, in the distance, the hills rolled off beyond the brick dorms, academic buildings and the ranchland and orchards that were used to teach hands-on classes to the majority of agriculture students.

He'd thought that getting away from the hotel and sitting here by the pool with some of his brothers at his old fraternity would clear his head, but nope.

He just kept thinking about earlier in the day, after Margot had tucked in her shirt and straightened out her clothes and hair.

She'd sauntered around the room, and he'd known that she was checking for a camera. Satisfied there was none, she'd gone over to her basket on the dresser and almost defiantly brought it over to him. He'd just stared at her while she'd let out an exasperated breath.

"You already know how this works," she said. "You just reach in and pick out a slip of paper."

Was she messing with him? Just a few minutes ago, she'd seemed ready to kick him to the curb for going too far with her.

Not knowing exactly what she was up to, he'd drawn a folded piece of paper from the basket. He barely even read the words before handing it back to her.

She'd taken one look at it, put the basket on the dresser again, grabbed a truffle and a croissant from the tray he'd put together and left the room.

But not before she'd flung one last comment over her shoulder.

"Nine o'clock, my room."

And that was it.

Had she just agreed to experience one of those eighty ways with him tonight?

As Clint mulled over the possibility, he was brought back to the present by an object hitting him in the shoulder. It didn't take him long to see what it was—a wet, spongy ball that some Phi Rho Mu pledges had been zinging at each other in the whirlpool in a game of close-quarter dodgeball.

Clint threw it right back at them, hitting a redheaded pledge in the chest.

All the older guys sitting in lounge chairs around the pool were entertained, including Riley. He was right next to Clint, wearing a baseball cap over his dark hair, protecting his Irish skin from the mild central California sun.

"Rise and shine, Barrows," he muttered.

So Riley had noticed he was a little out of it. Before Clint could explain why, all the brothers who were lounging at the side of the pool, whether they were part of the ten-year reunion or active, started barking orders at the pledges.

Clint hadn't been the only one who'd come to his college stomping grounds to relive old times during the reunion.

"Out of the cushy spa, scrubs!"

"Recite those stud numbers!"

"Into the big pool—*now!*"

Clint took a drink of his beer. It was as flat as his enthusiasm for joining in.

"Was that all we did back then?" he asked Riley as the other brothers surrounded the pledges. "Haze our underlings, drink beer all the time and generally act like idiots?"

"Pretty much." Riley set his bottle down on the concrete as he watched the pledges swim as many laps as the brothers told them to.

Clint glanced at Riley. Something wasn't sitting right with his friend today, either.

"Did the girls take Dani out this afternoon?" Clint asked, thinking that Riley's "something" probably had to do with his fiancée.

He shifted in his chair. "Dani's in the room, resting. I think she's looking at wedding stuff on our laptop. Margot and Leigh's enthusiasm seems to have gotten to her."

Clint recalled what Riley had told him the other day about not being able to give Dani the perfect wedding. Clearly, it was still eating away at him.

Now that Riley had started, he was on a roll. "There're times I wonder if Dani just isn't telling me how disappointed she is in how things have turned out with us. Margot and Leigh are helping her find reasonable alternatives to that grand wedding she always wanted, but…"

"But those alternatives aren't what you would give her if you could. You told me all about it."

Riley took a drink. He didn't have to answer.

Clint watched his brothers hazing those pledges, making them cling to the sides of the pool and kick their legs in a contest to see who lasted the longest. A thought hit him, just as that sponge ball had bopped into his shoulder earlier.

"You have a place for that wedding?" he asked Riley.

"Not so far."

Clint smiled. "Maybe I can at least help you out with that part."

He mentioned his ranch—the wide-open spaces, the grassy lawn, the guest cottages and the gazebo where his own parents had gotten hitched once upon a time.

When Clint was done, Riley was leaning forward in his chair, a big smile on his face.

Clint went back to his beer. Riley couldn't have missed how much he loved that ranch, and Clint didn't want to make a big deal out of it.

Mostly, though, he didn't want to think about how much it'd hurt to lose it.

"You'd go through all the trouble of having a major ruckus like a wedding on your spread?" Riley asked, instead of commenting on Clint's emotional slip.

"Of course. The twins are talking legal threats right now, but they won't be able to take the ranch away by the end of the year, when you were planning to get hitched, so why not?" He shrugged. "You know it's not a big deal. Besides, you've been there and you know it'd work for you."

They grinned at each other, friend to friend. Then Riley's smile got a little devilish. "Okay, I'll ask Dani about it. But let me know if there're any favors I can do for you—getting you some nice wine from my boss's vineyard, putting in a good word for you with Margot…"

No one will ever know, he'd told Margot about tonight.

No one. Not even their friends.

So he kept his end of the bargain. "Didn't you hear that she's planning to give me my money back on that basket?"

"She can't do that."

"I won't force her to do something she doesn't want to."

Riley looked disappointed for him. And, for all Clint knew, maybe tonight wouldn't be worth lying to his friend about, anyway. Was Margot going to pull the rug out from under him by leaving him stranded outside her door, horny and expectant? Would she initiate an even bigger joke if he got inside her room, set on revenge for the embarrassment she'd suffered all those years ago?

Hell, he'd take his chances after what'd happened with her earlier today. Thinking about it made his cock threaten to go stiff again.

Riley said, "Just so you know, there's been a lot of talk in this house from some of the visiting brothers. You sure have tongues wagging."

"Because of the basket."

"Because of you and Margot, together again. 'The fraternity stud and the unfortunate girl who got her pride dented by a camera.'"

Clint pushed back the brim of his hat. "Is it bad of me to wish that it was more than just her pride that was dented?"

"What do you mean?"

Maybe this would be a good time to shut up. But it wasn't as if Clint could go home and bounce this off his twin brothers. "I mean that I've always wondered if she got angry just about the camera…or if there was something more to it."

His friend waited, and when Clint didn't offer anything else, Riley said, "You can't say it, can you?"

What? That he thought Margot had nursed some hopes about what might've happened after finally admitting she was attracted to him? That she'd had a flicker of a deeper emotion, as he did, and wondered if their obvious attraction might turn into something more lasting?

Hell, no. Romantic what-ifs weren't his style. Had never been.

But today, after holding her, feeling her… It'd all come rushing back.

Maybe he really had pinned his hopes on something that had never materialized back then, thanks to that practical joke. Whatever potential there was between them had been destroyed.

And he'd been nicked good, too.

One of the fraternity brothers by the pool, Tyler Hague, had overheard their conversation.

"Is our studliest stud in love?" he called out, while hovering over a pool-bound pledge doing a series of jumping jacks. "Hate to tell you, Barrows, but Margot wasn't so thrilled about you buying her basket last night."

Laughter ensued around the pool. Hilarious.

But they hadn't seen her today with him.

His ego told him to crow about his earlier encounter with her, just as he might've bragged back in college about all the other women he'd kissed and dismissed. Yet somewhere along the line, he'd lost his taste for conquests, and it'd happened after Margot and the video.

They were all staring at Clint, waiting for him to come back with a confident retort.

He kicked back into his chair instead and said, "Margot and I have agreed to forget about the basket. There's nothing between us. Never has been, never will be."

His brothers good-naturedly offered some off-color remarks about Clint's manhood that he ignored, and they soon refocused their attention on the pledges, ordering them out of the pool and telling them to drink from some full red beer cups that a brother had brought over.

Clint looked away. It'd been good to visit the old house where he'd lived throughout most of his college career. It'd been nice to gaze at the wall of pictures—of brothers come and gone—and to give a heartfelt hug to Mother, a paid house mom who'd watched over them and still watched over a new generation of beer-guzzling kids.

But during this particular visit back to his old stomping grounds, Clint realized that there had to be something more than drinking and floating along from day to empty day.

He just wasn't sure what that something more was yet.

"If you wanted to win some brownie points with Margot," Riley said, getting to his feet, "I think you just scored."

Clint stayed silent. Riley didn't know it, but he intended to score a whole hell of a lot more tonight.

LATER THAT DAY, Margot was running on all cylinders, almost as if she'd eaten an entire bowl of raw sugar and she needed to burn it off.

Antsy. *Nervous.* Almost regretting that she had told

Clint to report to her at nine o'clock, after the reunion-closing dinner had been served downstairs.

If she were smart, she would just call off this fiasco-in-the-making, distancing herself from Clint altogether. How hard could it be, anyway, when tonight was the last official event of the reunion? She wouldn't ever have to see him again, wouldn't ever have to think of his cocky smile, his sure hands, his way of making her feel as if she were the only woman he'd ever touched in the way he'd touched her this afternoon.

But Margot didn't want to be smart about Clint Barrows. Not after the heights he'd taken her to with only a little foreplay.

Since Dani had opted to stay back at the hotel, Margot and Leigh had decided to get out and about, to see some of their college downtown haunts while they still could. Margot didn't mention that she actually had another agenda, and it had everything to do with the piece of paper Clint had pulled out of her basket.

Le Crazy Horse, Paris...

She told herself that she was in this merely for the fun as she and Leigh combed the tree-lined downtown streets, meandering in and out of the shops, some of which had survived the years, while others had been taken over by corporate chains.

When they came to The Boudoir, the lingerie shop that every Cal-U girl had visited at least once in her college career, it was just as kitschy and tempting as it had been when Margot was young. Back then every sex toy had made her and the girls giggle and every see-through nightie had been a romantic dream.

Margot managed to slyly purchase a couple of erotic items while Leigh perused the massage-lotion area. Back outside, they passed a new tavern that advertised

Red Bull drinks and Rave Night, a far cry from the country bar that used to thrive here.

"Were those booby tassels I saw you buy?" Leigh asked out of nowhere, her boot heels clicking on the concrete as they walked.

So much for secrecy. "Why would I need tassels?"

"Exactly my question. Because I'd think they wouldn't be so comfortable to wear. They seem too… jiggly."

"I know." Margot scoffed. "*I* don't wear tassels."

At least, she hadn't in the past. But she was rather looking forward to it tonight.

Too much, actually.

Leigh narrowed a glance at her. "And I saw some sexy bubble bath going into your bag, also."

"Do you have eyes in the back of your head or something?"

"Marg, you're just really bad at trying to be stealthy."

Nosy old biddy.

And Leigh wouldn't let up. "You told me that you canceled Clint's basket, but you didn't, did you?"

"Maybe I just want to take a nice bath tonight. Did you ever think of that?"

"Some bath. I've never used booby tassels for one of those."

Up ahead, Margot spied Alicia's Bridal Boutique, and a clear way to get out of this conversation came to her like an angelic chorus.

She grabbed Leigh's arm and steered her toward the store. "Check it out—we can do some reconnaissance work for Dani here."

"I don't know," Leigh said as she was pulled along. "She wasn't too happy about us butting in with the auction."

"But she warmed up to those wedding-gown pictures during breakfast."

Unwilling to take no for an answer—and to hear any more of Leigh's all-too-on-the-nose suspicions about Clint—Margot hauled her into the shop. A bell dinged at the door and a white puffy lace heaven of bridal finery welcomed them.

The clerk wasn't around, so Margot left Leigh and headed straight for the veils, choosing a flowered crown with a fall of tulle.

"Here we go," she said, pretending to wear it while showing Leigh. "Elegant and very Princess Grace-y."

Leigh grinned as she chose her own veil—a simple white flower with netting. She poised it on top of her head and to the side, making sure the netting came over one eye. "Do I look like Miranda Lambert at her wedding to Blake Shelton?"

"Better. There isn't a country singer in the world who could carry that off the way you do."

For a second, Leigh got a look on her face that was very un-Leigh. In fact, it was downright dreamy.

Margot put her veil back. Neither she nor Leigh had ever possessed illusions about getting married. But as she saw Leigh go to a mirror and look at herself with a starry-eyed gaze, she wondered if, somewhere along the way, Leigh had deserted her in the Single Girl Forever Sisterhood.

And… Well, it was lonely being abandoned like that, especially in the middle of a bridal store. But Margot had learned to be independent a long time ago, moving from place to place, never setting down roots or getting to know anyone—especially boys—on a deep level. Yes, she'd kissed her share of them, but there was always a distance that she felt, because she knew she would be leaving.

And things hadn't changed, even in college. She'd been comfortable being on her own, doing what she wanted to do, never being attached at the hip to a guy like some of her sorority sisters tended to be.

But now...

No, she wouldn't think of Clint. Why had he even popped into her head when she was just going to have a secret no-strings, this-one's-for-my-libido fling with him tonight? She'd scratch the itch that had been burning in her ever since that night in college, appeasing the curiosity of what his mouth would feel like on all the throbbing places on her body. She'd fill herself up with him as she'd filled herself with adventures her entire life, then go home, closing that chapter for good.

Wandering toward the gowns, Margot focused on Leigh as her friend checked herself out in the mirror, flushed.

"Are you thinking about the guy who bought your basket?" she asked.

That seemed to wake Leigh up, and she let out a belly laugh as she put her veil back on its rack. The laugh sounded a little hollow.

"I told you I don't ever get my hopes up about men," she said, her hand lingering on the veil one extra moment before she walked away. "I'm still just like you in that way, Marg."

Just like her.

Margot didn't like the sound of that, even if she'd made a career and a brand out of "independent woman adventures" with her books.

But it was as if something had dropped inside of her now—a little stone that fell and fell through the emptiness until it hit bottom, making a pinging splash that reverberated through her.

Leigh ambled around until she came to a tea-length gown. She tilted her head, as if picturing herself in it.

"Leigh," Margot said, without even realizing that she'd intended to talk. "Maybe I'm not the best example for anything."

It was on the tip of her tongue to tell Leigh how her glamorous life wasn't so glamorous these days. Without steady work or success, she wasn't sure how happy she could be or would be.

Leigh looked baffled. "Don't say that, Margot. You live under a lucky star, whether it comes to men or anything else, and I always thought how damned nice it'd be if I didn't have to work twice as hard to do everything you did so easily."

Margot swallowed. A confession was there, in her throat, but it had balled up, burning, waiting for her voice to utter the words.

But they never came.

Clint didn't bother to go down to the final dinner in the Golden Coast Ballroom. He was hungry for something else entirely, and he had no stomach for mere food.

He took a long, cold shower, then forced himself to sit in front of the TV, watching ESPN until five after nine.

He didn't want Margot to think he was too excited.

Still, before he left, he brushed his teeth one more time, put his Stetson on and went to his door. Then he backtracked, cursing under his breath, and grabbed that white negligee he'd bought earlier today for Margot, gathering all the soaps and lotions, too. He left the dressing screen, scarves and bamboo candle stand alone.

As he approached her room, he had a flashback to the night he'd brought Margot to his college room, never imagining that there was a camera set to record them. His veins tangled, just as they had back then.

Before he knew it, he was knocking on her door, waiting, thinking after a long second that, yeah, this was going to be a joke she'd created to exact her revenge, not only for all those years ago, but for today, too, when he'd been less than a gentleman with her.

Not that she hadn't enjoyed it.

Finally, the lock clicked and the door cracked open. It seemed to take forever.

He couldn't see her, but it was dim inside the room and music was playing, maybe from that computer he'd seen her using at breakfast with the girls.

The tune was slow and sultry, with an accordion and a woman's red-light voice.

Le Crazy Horse, Paris, he thought, the words from the note he'd drawn from Margot's basket flashing in his head like neon.

He pushed the door open slowly, and when he stepped into the room, the bathroom door was just closing.

Flickering candlelight showed through the open slit just before the door shut tight.

"I'll be ready in a minute." She was talking in a candlelit tone, as if she was waiting for him in the shadows.

As he went to put down the negligee and bath products on the dresser, he pictured what she might be wearing, what she was planning. Something tugged at him inside his belly, tightening him up.

So far this was no joke.

He heard the sound of water splashing against the tub inside the bathroom, and his knees nearly buckled.

Yet she kept him waiting.

And waiting.

He was just about ready to knock down the door when he heard the sound of the shower curtain being drawn, then her voice again.

"You can come in now…without your phone."

She was cautious about him filming this. "I don't have it on me."

"Good."

Playing it cool, he entered the bathroom. Candlelight flickered orange against the walls and, from behind the shower curtain, he saw light, too.

And a silhouette.

His mouth went dry.

Margot, every curve of her in smoky black shadow. Her hair was down around her shoulders, one hand resting on the back of her head as she stood in profile, accentuating her breasts.

Was she wearing a piece of lingerie that clung to her? He couldn't tell, but he leaned against the wall to keep himself from ripping the curtain aside and ruining the sensuous image.

Just enjoy, he thought. *It's the only night you'll be able to do it.*

"What's going on, Hemingway?" he asked, his voice thick as he teased her about being an English major, just as he used to. The scent of peaches wafted to him, making him dizzy.

"This is your first and only stop of eighty," she said, sassy as could be. "That's what's going on."

"What's this stop?"

He would play along. For now. Let her feel the power

that had been taken away from her with that camera a decade ago.

She touched the curtain, and he sucked in a breath.

"Don't you remember what that slip of paper said?" she asked. "You drew it from the basket only a few hours ago."

"Humor me."

She laughed again, shifting so that her silhouetted hips swayed to the other side. "Le Crazy Horse, Paris. Do you know anything about it?"

"I think I know everything I need to." *Let's get on with it,* his body screamed.

"That's not how we play this," she said, swaying again, her hips so ripe, so in need of touching and caressing.

He settled in for her brand of verbal foreplay. "Then tell me."

She sounded satisfied. "The club was started up in 1951 by Alain Bernardin in Paris. He was an artist with avant-garde tastes and an appreciation for women. Le Crazy Horse is known mainly for its burlesque—racy acts with musical numbers and humor thrown in for relief."

"Relief from what?"

She pulled on the far side of the shower curtain just enough that it offered a peek of the wall tile, and that was all.

Why did it seem that she was always offering a tiny glimpse of herself, and not just in a physical sense?

Why, dammit, did he want more?

But she was already speaking.

"What kind of relief do you think I'm talking about?" she asked. "If you get a rise out of every female act they perform, wouldn't you need a break?"

Speaking of which… His jeans were getting awful tight.

The water swished against the sides of the tub again as she began to move to the music—an enticing blend of the singer's come-hither voice and the lazy pull of that accordion.

Clint watched her for a while, imagining what she might do if he reached behind the curtain and touched her. He hadn't seen her face this afternoon when he'd brought her to orgasm, and the more he watched her dance for him in silhouette, the more he wanted to know if she had closed her eyes when she came, what her mouth had looked like shaped around a cry of ecstasy.

What she felt when he got close like this.

When the song ended, another one began.

"Do you know who Gypsy Rose Lee is?" she asked. "Or Lili St. Cyr?"

He was dying here. "No."

"They were famous in the striptease world and a big influence on Dita Von Teese. She's one of the biggest names in the business, and she played Le Crazy Horse not too long ago."

He was just about to destroy that curtain when she finally pulled at it, wrapping it over her body so it molded every curve of her figure.

Her face… God, he hadn't realized it, but he'd wanted to see her face so badly, and the sight of those pale eyes and dark lashes and red lips didn't disappoint. It gutted him, pierced him through with a lust so strong that he could barely stand it.

"Ms. Von Teese," Margot said, "does a little number called '*Le Bain*.'"

Clint had barely squeaked by the foreign-language requirement in college—he'd taken a semester of French just because he knew a lot of romantic-minded girls would be in the class—and he remembered what *le bain* meant.

The bath.

Margot's gaze locked to his as she pushed the curtain all the way to the side.

His lungs cut off his air supply when he saw her standing in front of a candle in the corner. She was wearing a pink chiffon slip that was so tight it left very little to the imagination. Her arms were slim, toned, her legs going on forever. Under the material, he could've sworn that she was wearing tassels over her breasts.

She bent to the bubble-laced water, still looking at him, then splashed a handful over her chest.

As it drizzled down into her cleavage and dampened the material over her breasts, he laughed softly, taking off his hat and tossing it outside the bathroom.

"Don't do this to me," he said, half kidding. Because he liked what she was doing, even though it was one long tease that was making his balls blue.

But, being Margot, she did it again.

Two scoops this time, one over each breast.

He couldn't see the tips of them through the more padded parts, but the water plastered the rest of the sheer lingerie to her stomach, her belly, hinting at the lace panties she was wearing.

Those were getting wet, too, droplets clinging to the thighs exposed by her short gown.

"Dammit, Margot," he murmured.

As if driven on by those words, she turned her back to him, once again swaying to the slow music. She reached to the front of her slip, undoing the buttons there. Then, inch by inch, she lowered the material from her shoulders, exposing her bare back.

He leaned against the wall, gritting his teeth.

Smiling—maddeningly, teasingly, totally knowing that she was in control of him—she allowed the slip to drop to her waist.

The slope of her back drove him wild, but he didn't show it.

"What comes next?" he asked.

She turned toward him, revealing her breasts. They were tipped with silver tassels that she touched, stroked.

He wiped a hand down his face. So close to seeing more of her, yet so far. The mounds of her breasts were beautiful to him, perfect, begging for his hands and fingers and mouth. And as she wiggled out of the rest of her gown, tossing it to the tiled floor, he yearned to relieve her of those lace panties, too.

She palmed more water, but now she slid her hands up her legs, wetting them, allowing the liquid to roll down her skin.

"I think," she said, still leaning over, giving him a good view of her breasts, "you like this trip so far."

"I've always liked," he said. "I've always wanted."

He just wouldn't tell her how much.

He took a step forward without even thinking, but she held up a hand and shook a finger at him playfully.

"We've got a long way to go, Stud."

She reached for the handheld showerhead and turned on the water, her smile all-knowing.

So seductive that he didn't know if he could last as long as this trip would take.

7

THEY SAID THE first rule of striptease was that you can touch him, but he can't touch you.

At least, that was what Margot had seen and heard in the clubs she'd been in, like Le Crazy Horse. She'd written about the girls there and everywhere—women who seduced men with long looks and suggestive dances.

And now, as Clint Barrows watched her, she became one of those girls—someone who was wanted by a man more than anything else in the world. She could see it in his eyes, the wanting. Could practically feel it rising above the bath-steeped humidity in the room as the candles flickered.

She recognized the same yearning look from that night so long ago. Naked need in his gaze and… Now that she was in the moment, she remembered there'd been something else she'd seen in him that had scared her, even while making her heart beat with the same stilted, unfamiliar rhythm that it was right now.

But, at this moment, she wasn't that Margot, was she? She wasn't the girl from college who'd had an awkward incident with him that had sent her bursting out of a dim room, leaving him behind and darkening his name in her personal history. And even though the thought of becoming someone else for the night—someone who had no worries about her future and lived for the day—appealed to Margot, it was actually the only way she was going to be able to get through this seduction.

The only way her pride was going to stay intact while her body had a holiday.

As the water sprayed from the showerhead she held, the peach-scented bubbles from the bath clung to her calves, water beading on her skin. She ran her fingers down her soaked panties, up over her belly, then between her legs.

His gaze followed, a muscle in his jaw pulsing as he kept leaning against the wall, otherwise as casual as you please.

But that ticking muscle told her that he was steamed up inside, no matter how cool he looked.

"Imagine," she said as the music kept playing. "My hands are your hands, touching me, making me hot."

She slipped the showerhead inside her panties, dousing herself with water, leaving the lace clinging to her. Pressing back against the wall, she kept showering herself, stroking herself.

Hungry. He looked hungry enough to stop this show altogether and have his way with her. His gaze was burning with it.

But so was she. Her juices were swamping her, her breath coming faster and faster, especially when she pulled her panties away from her so he could see a bit more—but not much more—while she aimed the stream of water at her most sensitive parts.

She hauled in a hard breath, arching into the spray as it tickled her clit.

Then she whispered, "Your hands and fingers feel so good on me."

She closed her eyes, maybe because she didn't want to look at him, to see the reality of what she was doing. She and Clint Barrows—a scenario she would have fought tooth and nail before today. Her pride wouldn't let her forget it.

But here she was.

And it *was* good.

She opened her eyes to see him grinning now, starting to unbutton his shirt.

"Uh-uh," she said, shaking her head while still massaging herself, building herself up to a point where she wouldn't be able to even talk or make intelligible sounds much longer, just like yesterday, when she'd pleasured herself to thoughts of him.

A fantasy.

Not real. Never real with him.

"There's been enough teasing," he said. The candlelight laved the tanned skin of his muscled chest, the bunched abs.

As he shrugged off his shirt, a pierce of desire made her stifle a moan.

Her nipples went hard, sensitive as hell, aching to feel his chest against hers.

And he noticed, his gaze eating her up.

He laughed, low and wicked, as he undid the top button of his fly, where a bulge strained against his jeans.

Something like panic shot threw her. *She* was the one who would set the pace today. She flicked the showerhead in his direction, spraying some water at him.

"You need to cool off," she said.

He only laughed again, leaving his fly slightly open at the top, where a thin trail of golden hair disappeared.

The sight of it excited her even more.

As he removed his boots and socks, she took her hand out of her panties.

"I think you need to be reminded," she said, gesturing to her entire body, "that this isn't for you. You can look, but you can't touch."

"You sure about that, Tolstoy?"

Before she could be mildly impressed with his continued recall of Literature 101—how many authors' names would he call her before this was over?—he undid another button on his fly.

"When you were touching yourself," he asked, "were you thinking of how much better it'd be if I was doing it? If I was inside you, making you want to cry out like you did earlier today?"

She would never admit any of that to him. Hell, she'd spent the beginning of the night laughing downstairs at the dinner and acting like nothing was bothering her—surely she could do that with Clint, too.

"You think a lot of yourself," she said. "Don't you, Stud?"

"You know what I think a lot about?"

Another button, undone.

Another part of her, undone, as he took a step toward the tub.

He lowered his voice. "I think a lot about you. I haven't been able to stop since I laid eyes on you again."

She could barely find the oxygen to speak. "That's because you want what you can't have."

When he got close enough, he reached out, hooking a finger in her panties, tugging at them, and it was as if she had turned to hot water herself, near boiling.

"You want me to have it," he said, slipping her panties down an inch, so that her hip was exposed.

She was pulsing for him, between her legs, in her chest. Was she going to let him have it?

Yes, she thought. *Hell, yes.*

But only when she said so.

As he pulled down her panties more, she covered herself with a hand. Another rule of striptease—hide your bits.

Keep teasing.

He worked the material down her legs, and she allowed him to do it. She even stepped out of the lace without being urged, watching him throw it carelessly behind him.

He glanced up at her with those light blue eyes— eyes that could talk her into anything. A gaze that had probably talked any number of girls into more than they should've given him.

For a long time, she'd been determined never to be one of those girls—not with any man. She was better than that.

But as she saw how much he wanted her, she knew that it would be fine if it were on her terms.

When he stood, she reached for his fly, undoing the last button. Then she took him into her hand—hard, long, stiff. Everything she'd never gotten ten years ago.

All for her.

She caressed him, up, down, so slowly that he shut his eyes, clenching his jaw.

"Maybe *you're* the one who wants to be inside me more than anything," she said. "You're thinking about it right now, feeling how you'd slip into me, coming inside me over and over again."

She circled a thumb over his tip, and he groaned low in his throat.

"Just how long do you think you're going to last?" she asked, ruthless.

"All night if I have to."

Oh, really? Now who was wielding the power?

Ramped up, she decided to tease him even more, skimming her fingertips underneath his shaft until she got to his balls. She toyed with him, watching how his nipples went hard, how a vein in his throat strained.

"You're not going to last another second," she whispered.

It was a challenge the adventurous side of her wanted him to accept.

And he did.

Everything happened at once—his eyes opened, his fingers locked around her wrist, and before she knew it, he was in the tub with her, splashing water with such force that he doused the candle in the corner.

Her pulse was nearly deafening as he lifted her, bringing her against the wall, gently yet firmly removing one tassel from her breast before latching on to her with his mouth, sucking at her until the pleasant throb between her legs became unbearably painful.

In a good way, she thought as she wound her fingers through his thick hair. In one of eighty good ways....

As he worked at a nipple, his fingers sought the other, taking off the tassel, then playing with her as mercilessly as she'd played with him, bringing her to a peak so quickly that her mind couldn't catch up.

But he had to know that he was driving her crazy, and he looked up at her with those hungry eyes and a cruel grin.

Who's not gonna last? that grin seemed to ask.

She heard the answer echoing in the back of her mind. *Me. I can't stop myself with you, damn you.*

She yanked down his jeans, bringing them around his hips as she slid down the tiled wall to the bath. He stopped her, reaching into one of his pockets for a condom, then worked off his jeans the rest of the way, discarding them with a wet thud on the floor.

Once she was sitting in the water, warm, frothy bubbles popped over her everywhere as she watched him sheathe himself, then kneel in front of her in the bath, lifting one of her legs over his arm.

Open to him. She was so damned open, the water lapping at her, once again making her want to scream.

He only made it worse when he teased her with his tip, running it down between her folds.

"Is this what you want?" he asked. "Are you still playing a game?"

It would always be a game with them, nothing more.

But even as she thought it, that inner sinking sensation—the stone hitting water and causing ripples—hit her.

She ignored it, wiggling under him, giving as good as she was getting from him.

"You want it more," she said.

Another laugh, gritty and amused. "I want it a hell of a lot."

And he drove into her, as if to show her that he wasn't going to deny anything—not his lust, not the lengths to which she'd driven him.

Not her.

She gasped, digging her nails into his arm, water slick over his skin and muscle as he rammed into her again.

Bathwater sloshed over the sides of the tub as she moved with him at every thrust, her other hand planted in his hair while she insisted on dictating the pace.

He didn't seem to mind—not even when she demanded that she be on top, forcing him beneath her, riding him, causing frenetic waves to slap the tile floor.

She braced a hand on the wall, working him, feeling him go deep inside her, closing her eyes again as patterns of light ricocheted wildly across her field of vision.

At first she didn't know what she saw in them, all of the shapes unfamiliar, just as foreign as what she'd seen in his eyes back in college, just as confusing as the strange emotions that had nipped at her as he'd kissed her, caressed her.

And now, they were back, but intensified.

Flashes of heat. Swirls. Jags of lightning…

The rumble of oncoming thunder in her body.

It started in her clit, gathered in her belly, pushing out with such energy that the orgasm came like a bolt out of the blue, hitting her, rattling her, making her take such a needle-sharp breath that she didn't think she'd ever be able to breathe again.

He wasn't far behind, though, and when he came, he said her name.

"Margot…"

Not an English-major nickname, not the name of a famous author, just…her.

The sound of it melted off the walls like beaded steam, slipping down like drops.

Slipping into her as if finding someplace it truly belonged.

AFTERWARD, CLINT watched her just as longingly as when he'd watched her perform the striptease.

Watched her push back a hank of hair that had come to cover her face while she climaxed. Watched her watch him, then catch a breath, looking away.

After that, he wasn't sure what happened. He just knew for certain that she was piecing herself together while she climbed out of the tub, water sluicing down every angle of her beautiful, long body before she grabbed a towel from the rack and started to dry off. He watched her as she wrapped that towel around herself, hiding everything from his gaze, before she walked out of the bathroom without another word.

He'd stayed in the tub a little longer, reveling in the aftermath, satiated.

That's what he was, right? Satiated? Sure, the pit of his belly ached for more. And, yeah, he hadn't been lying when he'd told her that he could last all night, because he was ready to go again.

And again.

But he was feeling something else, and he was afraid to look at it too closely, because this was it. One night only. A last hurrah at a reunion.

Obviously, she wouldn't let this go any further. She'd made her point to him already—that she'd won some kind of contest between them—and that was good enough for her.

The longer he sat in that bath, the more her attitude bothered him.

He got out of the tub. The water had gotten cold, anyway.

After he wound a towel around his hips, he found Margot by the window, the curtains shut. She'd turned off the music and turned on a light, but if she thought that the glare would wipe away the fantasy of what had gone on in the tub, she was dead wrong.

She was just as desirable in reality, with that towel wrapped around her and the ends of her lustrous hair plastered to her skin. And even with her back to him as she went through her suitcase, he couldn't deny that he'd seen that all-consuming light in her eyes when he'd been inside her.

"I haven't gone on a lot of trips in my lifetime," he said, "but I doubt there's one that would top where I just went."

Her shoulders stiffened as she held up a nightshirt for her inspection. Was she about to shoo him out so she could go to bed, dismissing him?

Well, it wasn't as if he hadn't gracefully put an end to more than a few nights like that himself.

"You must not take many vacations." She sounded so cool and collected.

Something about her tone made him angry. Okay, maybe not angry, but it tweaked that part of him that Margot always seemed to rile up.

The part of him that no one else ever got to.

He rested his hip against a dresser, crossing his arms over his chest. "You're the traveler. I'm the small-towner who likes where he's at."

"Then this should be enough excitement to last you."

Burn.

"You know," he said, not taking her words to heart, "there are way more slips of paper in that basket of yours. I'd hate for all your hard work to go to waste." He jerked his chin toward the soaps and lotions he'd brought over. The pretty white negligee. "And all these things I bought this morning? They can't just sit here."

"Use them on the next girl who comes along."

Could there be more to her attitude than he'd first thought?

"You're not pissed at me because you finally gave in, are you?" he asked.

In immediate hindsight, maybe this hadn't been the right subject to broach at the moment.

She turned around, her posture ramrod-straight. She held that nightshirt in front of her like a shield. "*I* gave in? As you might recall, you were pretty easy."

"I can't say you're wrong about that."

His carefree comment seemed to take the steam out of her argument—and Lord knew it looked as if she was ready for one. It didn't take a college graduate to know that this was her way of distancing herself.

She let the nightshirt fall to the bed. "I don't know. I'm just… It was fun, okay? It was a nice night. Let's not ruin it by analyzing it."

"Nice and fun. I guess that's one way of putting it." *Mind-blowing, earth-moving...* Those were other ways.

"You're no stranger to fun," she said.

"No, I'm not." He moved away from the dresser, his body drawn toward her. "I'm just wondering why it'd be a bad idea for us to have fun all night. After all, I didn't see any limitations on how many trips I'd get when I bought the basket."

"It was a one-time thing."

He decided to play this from a different angle. "You're right. It was nice and fun. I'm sure we can be adults about this and we won't get awkward when we see each other again."

She frowned. "We're seeing each other again?"

"You didn't think I'd skip Dani and Riley's wedding, did you?"

"It's entirely possible to avoid people at weddings."

"Well, I hear you're pretty involved with the planning, and since Dani and Riley are thinking about getting married on my ranch…"

Her eyes widened. "What're you talking about?"

He didn't need to tell her that it was only an idea that he'd floated by Riley this afternoon. "I offered up my ranch for the wedding. It's something that might put us in some amount of proximity, Margot."

Even when she doubled her frown, she was the most gorgeous woman he'd ever seen.

"Oh, come on," he said. "Don't tell me you'll be able to resist checking my place out with Dani and hanging around to offer decorating tips. I know she'll ask you and Leigh to do that, since you're the Three Musketeers."

"You did this on purpose, didn't you?"

"Strategized to have the wedding on my property just so I could see you again?" He shrugged. "I only made a kind gesture to one of *my* good friends."

"Don't twist my words."

"Okay." He comfortably crossed his arms over his chest. "I take it back—you *didn't* mean that I wanted to somehow lure you to my ranch so we could have more fun times together. But now that I think about it, that *is* a real good plan."

"You're impossible."

"I thought you said I was easy." He grinned.

Clearly, there wouldn't be any more going around the girl tonight—not with the mood she was in. But, even if Clint had to wear bath-soaked jeans back to his room, he'd gotten what he'd wanted from her, wasn't that right?

So why did he feel so…empty?

Before she could launch into a real argument, he sauntered back to the bathroom, managed to get into his wet clothes, picked up his boots and went to the door.

"Night, Margot," he said, tipping his hat to her. "I'll be seeing you."

"Don't count your weddings before they hatch."

Although it didn't sound like an endearment, he took it as one as he opened the door and risked a glance behind him, finding her watching him with a glimmer in her eye that told him she just might be looking forward to seeing him again, no matter what she said.

THE ROAD AHEAD of Dani and Riley stretched well into the darkness, illuminated by the headlights of his truck.

Dani, who was full from the subpar hotel banquet food, as well as all the socializing from the reunion, was just drifting off to sleep with Riley at the wheel when her phone played an ancient song from the '80s.

"Girls Like Me." Margot's ringtone.

Dani hopped on it, automatically pressing the speakerphone button. "You still back at the hotel?"

"I told you at the dinner that I decided to stay an extra night."

Funny thing. Riley had said that Clint was staying over, too.

She exchanged a glance with him, and he cracked a grin, his hand resting comfortably on the steering wheel as they zoomed along.

"Am I on speakerphone?" Margot asked.

"Nope."

Dani made a face at Riley, who put a finger to his lips. She shook her head, telling him that she was going to take this one in private.

After she pressed the button and put the phone to her ear, she asked, "So…anything going on in the hotel?"

"Nothing major."

Dani had known Margot a long time, and she could pinpoint when her friend was dancing around something.

"Did you and anyone…?" she started to ask.

"*Hell,* no."

Dani smiled, because Margot was protesting too much. Riley grinned as he guessed Margot's answer.

Maybe someday she would spill the beans about Clint, but it wouldn't be tonight.

"What I'm calling about," Margot said, "is a rumor I heard. Are you and Riley thinking about having your wedding on Clint Barrows's ranch?"

Dani mouthed to Riley, *"Ranch,"* then answered. "He mentioned it to me today, and I think it's a fantastic idea."

She thought she heard Margot mutter, "Crap."

"Riley's seen Clint's spread," Dani said, "but I'd like it if you and Leigh would check his place out with me. I need people who can look at it with wedding bells in mind."

Truthfully, Dani liked Clint. He put a light in Margot's eyes. He'd *always* made Margot act a little differently when he was in the room, not that she would ever cop to that.

"Are you sure about having Leigh and me out there with you for a look-see?" Margot asked. "We don't want to interfere…."

"Haven't you been doing that all along?"

Margot laughed. "All right. You've got me."

"I've got you for a visit to the ranch? If you're not busy, Riley and I were talking about this weekend."

Dani could just picture Margot softly banging her head against a wall.

"There's really no other place on earth you can have a wedding?" Margot asked.

"The price is right, baby. Plus, it sounds beautiful at

YOUR PARTICIPATION IS REQUESTED!

Dear Reader,

Since you are a lover of romance fiction – we would like to get to know you!

Inside you will find a short Reader's Survey. Sharing your answers with us will help our editorial staff understand who you are and what activities you enjoy.

To thank you for your participation, we would like to send you 2 books and 2 gifts – **ABSOLUTELY FREE!**

Enjoy your gifts with our appreciation,

Pam Powers

SEE INSIDE FOR READER'S SURVEY

For Your Romance Reading Pleasure...

YOUR READER'S SURVEY
"THANK YOU" FREE GIFTS INCLUDE:
▶ 2 Harlequin® Blaze™ books
▶ 2 lovely surprise gifts

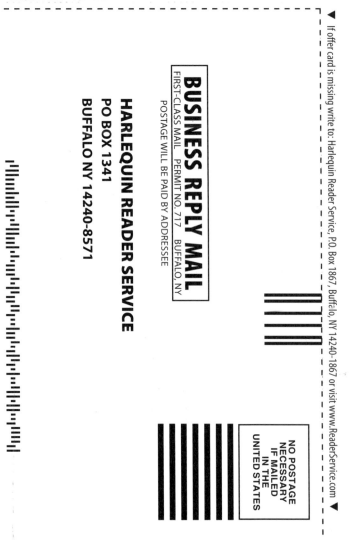

Clint's place, and there's enough room to accommodate everyone we want to invite."

A pause crackled over the connection, and if that wasn't enough to convince Dani that something had gone on with Margot and Clint this weekend, nothing ever would.

"Dani," Margot said. "You know I'd do anything for you."

"Even this?"

"Even this. I mean, what's the big deal, anyway, right? I had to see Clint Barrows *this* weekend and I got through it. I can do it again."

If that's how you want it, Margot. "I'm sure you can."

Margot blew out a breath. It was the closest she would ever come to an admission.

After they said their goodbyes and hung up, Dani rested her head against the seat.

"So?" Riley asked.

So what should she say? She'd just been thinking about all Margot's adventures, and how she and Clint might've had a real good one tonight.

Why hadn't *she* ever been able to have an adventure?

Because I'm too boring, Dani thought. *Too...me.* Always needing someone else—sorority sisters, a perpetual fiancé—and never a woman who sought out excitement on her own. Even sex with Riley was tender, sweet. But there'd never been *adventures.*

Maybe that was because Dani had always been afraid of feeling too much, like her mom had felt for her dad before he'd stepped out on her and they'd split up, becoming shells of their old selves.

She finally answered Riley's question. "I definitely think they had a moment."

"Clint and Margot?"

"It had to happen sometime this weekend."

She thought of what Margot might do if she were in a car with Clint, how they probably wouldn't be able to keep their hands off each other.

Adventures.

Why *not* her?

Slowly, she reached over to Riley, traced a finger over the side of his leg.

He smiled down at her, apparently expecting nothing more than a simple touch that said "I love you."

Something bent inside of her, like it was turning around, and she slid her hand up to the top of his thigh, toward his penis.

No. His *cock.*

The car jerked toward the side of the road.

"Jeez, Dani," he said, chuckling and righting the wheel.

She liked his shock, so she did it again, running her fingers over the bulge in his jeans, squeezing gently.

This time, he took her hand in one of his, brought it up to his mouth, kissed the back of it.

Her heart contracted, even though she knew that he hadn't exactly rejected her. He was just Riley and she was just Dani, and they had been best friends who'd turned to lovers.

That was the only time they'd surprised each other.

As Riley held her hand to his heart, his eyes on the straight road ahead, Dani thought about how Margot and Leigh had tried to raise money for her wedding, how everyone still saw her as that steady, dependable, romantic sorority sister nicknamed "Hearts."

Maybe it was high time for some surprises.

8

A WEEK HAD never passed more slowly for Clint, but when Margot's trendy Prius finally pulled into the long graveled driveway that led to his ranch house near Visalia, about a half hour away from Cal-U, he somehow stayed cool.

Dani, who'd been sitting next to him on the living room's cowhide sofa, popped out of her seat when she saw Margot through the window. She touched her hair self-consciously, probably because she'd gotten most of it chopped off this week in what she'd called a "modern bob," which basically meant that one side of her red curls now came to her chin while the other was a little longer.

"Finally!" she said, taking off in the direction of the front door.

From the chair next to Clint, Riley got up, too. As he watched Dani disappear from the room, he wore a look that was part affection, part puzzlement.

"Still getting used to the new fiancée?" Clint asked.

Riley sighed, then shrugged while ambling in the

direction of the entryway. "Even if she got a haircut on a whim, she's still my Dani."

When Clint glanced out the window again, he saw Margot getting out of her car and embracing Dani. His heartbeat did a strange jig in his chest, and he wondered why he was feeling something there when it should've been limited to his nethers.

He'd sincerely missed her, he thought. And in spite of all the work he'd been faced with after leaving the cutting horse operation during the reunion, he'd actually felt kind of bored without her around.

But it was just because of the sex.

Only the sex.

He walked to his foyer, then exited onto the porch with its hickory-wood chairs and tables and gliding swing, then down the few steps to the stone-lined entry path that led to the parked vehicles.

"Let me take a look at you," Margot was saying, holding Dani away from her as Riley lingered nearby.

Lightheartedly, Dani primped for her, showing off that stylish new hairdo.

Margot's smile was a million watts. "You look amazing!"

Clint couldn't stop gazing at her as something in his chest flared. Rays of energy beamed everywhere in him.

Weird.

As Margot linked arms with Dani, she sent a subtle wink at Riley, who ran a hand through his dark hair and returned the grin.

Finally, Margot glanced at Clint, and he casually nodded in greeting, as if his world wasn't being shaken.

"Good to see you, Margot," he said. How about that. He didn't sound affected by her at all.

But from the way she gave him a too-polite smile, he suspected that she was still in argument-mode from last weekend, when she'd pretty much told him that the sex had been good, but *bye-bye.*

"Good to see you, too," she said. "Thanks for having us here."

Riley cleared his throat, snagging everyone's attention. "Looks like it's just the four of us, then."

Margot seemed relieved to break gazes with Clint. "Leigh told you she has reshoots for one of her cooking episodes?"

Riley and Dani nodded as Clint said, "Did she ever hear anything about the secret admirer who won her basket?"

Margot's gaze widened ever so slightly, as if baskets were the last thing she wanted to be talking about with him around.

Dani answered for her. "The only thing Leigh found out was that he should be back in the country by the end of the month, and he'll be contacting her then."

"Out of the country?" Clint wondered which fraternity brother did all that traveling, plus had a lot of play money. He couldn't come up with a name offhand. "I guess he's a jet-setter, just like Margot."

It was as if, once again, he'd said something that didn't sit right with her, because her smile didn't reach her eyes.

"I'm just a writer who likes doing what she does. That's all."

Why did she seem a little…sad?

Dani started pulling her away from the car. "Clint promised us a beautiful sunset, so you're just in time to see it at the gazebo where Riley and I could take our vows. You ready for a tour?"

"Show me the way."

The women took off, leaving Riley and Clint to walk after them. Clint didn't object, because it gave him ample opportunity to enjoy the way Margot's rear filled the back of her dark knit dress.

What kind of panties was she wearing today? Lace? Nothing at all?

As they passed the cottages where the original owners had lived before the main house was built, Dani pointed to the west. The tops of the ranch hands' bunkhouses met the horizon off in the distance.

"The working part of the ranch is over that way," Clint said. "Near enough so that your wedding guests could go for a horseback ride if they want, but far enough so this living area doesn't have too much of that ranch…"

"Aroma?" Margot asked.

"Exactly."

Dani was a small-town girl, but she hadn't grown up on a farm or ranch like most Phi Rho Mu members had. She was a bit of an outsider, and that's probably why she got along with the biggest outsider of them all— Margot.

And that's why Clint had been so attracted to her, he thought. Because she'd always been different. Challenging.

His blood pumped as he watched the breeze toy with the layers of Margot's long hair, but then, when he thought about how she'd just about vowed they'd never get together again, his pulse mellowed.

Strangest of all, his heart actually felt heavy.

It didn't take long to get to the gazebo, which was surrounded by autumn-hued bushes with anemic leaves. Margot immediately went to them.

Dani said, "Clint told us we could plant flowers for

the late spring. Since we're having a bigger wedding now, we decided to move the date back."

"That'll be gorgeous." While Margot surveyed the rectangular pine gazebo, that sad smile Clint had noticed earlier tipped the corners of her mouth. "This is absolutely perfect, Dani."

"I think so, too."

As they stood there, still linking arms, Clint had another rogue thought: yes, this was somehow near to perfect, seeing Margot on his property, in front of the gazebo where his parents had gotten married.

While he tried to figure himself out, Margot climbed the steps to the gazebo's spacious floor.

"Are you going to use the catering company you work for?" she asked. "Aren't they too far away to be convenient?"

Dani glanced at the group, seeming anxious about what she was going to say next. She walked over to Riley, touching his arm. "So…about the catering. I won't be using my company because… Well, I've actually been thinking…" Now she looked up at Riley. "I'm not sure how much longer I'll be working with them."

When Riley glanced down at her, it was obvious this was the first time he was hearing this.

Margot piped up. "Come again?"

Dani tucked a strand of her new, bobbed hair behind an ear and smiled at Riley. "I've been thinking about quitting." She added in a lowered voice to Riley, "It's been on my mind, hon."

Silence flapped in the air until Riley turned around, shaking his head as he walked away. Dani offered an apologetic glance to Margot and Clint before she went after him.

That left the two of them standing there, awkward as hell.

Clint spoke. "Who knew those two were capable of a disagreement?"

"The hard feelings won't last long. Riley and Dani are one of those couples who don't really have problems."

Not problems you can see clearly, anyway.

That part of it went unspoken between them.

As they waited, all but shuffling their boots, Margot got that sad distance in her eyes again, as if she couldn't help keeping her mind off what was troubling her.

Then she sighed. "I suppose I should get settled."

"Right." It wasn't as if they were friends and he could ask her what was wrong.

So he led her back to the ranch house, a canyon of tension between them.

It'd been a semi-awkward dinner, with Riley as unreadable as a closed book and Dani filling the silence by chatting away about her future plans for her own catering company.

Lord knew what had gotten into her, Margot thought, but she could just imagine the private conversation that'd gone on between Dani and Riley after that minibombshell at the gazebo.

"You're going to quit?" he probably would've said once they were alone. *"Where did this come from, Dani?"*

Fortunately, Margot had gotten the opportunity to ask Dani the same question while Clint and Riley had bonded over grilling steaks outside and Margot had helped Dani in the kitchen with twice-baked potatoes,

Caesar salad, plus mushrooms stuffed with spinach and topped by a béchamel sauce.

She hadn't gotten much out of Dani, though.

"Everyone and everything changes," she had said simply. "Remember last weekend when you told me that I was capable of running my own business, and I just hadn't taken the opportunity to try it? Well, that stuck with me, Margot. It made me rethink where I'm going and where I've been."

Margot ran her gaze over Dani's saucy haircut, but didn't say anything more. Quitting a job and pursuing a new business was a serious turn of events for anyone, but the issue was between Dani and Riley. And, until her friend wanted advice or feedback, Margot would let them work it out.

AFTER DINNER, DANI shooed everyone out of the kitchen, preferring to clean up "like the totally efficient home ec machine" she said she was, so Margot wasn't sure what to do with herself. She was hardly tired, though, so she retreated to the porch, where night had already fallen across the clear California country sky, stars winking down.

She chose to sit in a gliding herringbone swing and leaned back, finally breathing for the first time that day. It'd been a rough one. Yesterday, she'd gotten news from her agent that her publishing house hadn't merely decided to refuse any future contracts with her, but they had actually told her to forget about fulfilling the final book on her present agreement. She couldn't stop worrying about it.

I'm an official, utter failure, she thought. And where was there for a failure to go now? She heard the door open, and she straightened up.

It was Clint, holding two crystal shot glasses with golden liquid, backlit by the warm illumination from the foyer.

His boot steps thudded on the planks as he walked toward her, and her heart imitated the sound with tiny booms.

The two of us alone...Le Crazy Horse...a bubble bath...

"Nightcap?" he asked, handing her a glass.

"What did you bring me?" It'd been asinine to think that she wouldn't find herself alone with him again. But this time, she would stay strong.

Even if she was already going weak, just from smelling the clover and hay on his skin.

Something in her chest seemed to expand because he was near, and she shooed the sensation away.

"It's a liqueur," he said. "St. Germain. They say it's really rich, made from elderflowers."

"You've never had it before?"

"First time for everything, even for a fellow like me."

She couldn't help laughing at that and took the glass in hand.

He said, "I figured you all might like it."

"I've had it before, and it's wonderful. Thank you." She almost tacked on a "stud" at the end of the sentence but bit her tongue before old, flirting habits could take over.

No need to flirt with him when they'd finally gotten each other out of their systems.

He sat next to her in a rustic chair. Couldn't he leave her alone to wallow in her misery with a fine libation, just as if she were a poet with her absinthe?

He'd doffed his hat earlier, and his hair was a mess.

Damn him for that, too, because she found it adorable in a dumb, schoolgirl-crush way.

"So," he said.

"So." She searched for words. "How about the drama you've got on your ranch? And we haven't even come to a wedding yet."

"Are you talking about the girl with the new hair-cut?" He jerked his chin toward the door, indicating Dani. "I'm leaving her and Riley to work everything out."

"I can't blame her for flailing around a little. She's getting married and making a huge life change. I think this is her version of cold feet."

Why was she talking so much?

Clint only nodded as he took a sip of the St. Germain. When she caught herself aping his movements, she paused. Then she thought, *Screw it,* and drank away, letting the thick warmth of the liqueur travel down her throat and through her limbs.

What to talk about now? It wasn't as if they'd ever had a normal conversation. But here, under the stars, at his home, normal seemed…well, normal. It was nice to be someplace comfy like this. She'd never really sat on a porch with someone before and felt like she didn't want to rush off anywhere.

"You've got a great place here," she finally said. "It'll be a fabulous location for the wedding. You were right about that."

"Thanks."

"Your brothers don't care that you offered it to Dani and Riley?"

He took his shot glass and held it up, absently look-ing through it, as if to inspect the golden nectar. Offhandedly, he said, "I'm going to assume Riley told you much more about Jeremiah and Jason than I thought."

She was skating on thin ice here, and she wasn't sure if it would hold. Why had she even mentioned his brothers?

Out of anxiety, she thought. Out of the pure, scary adrenaline freeze of trying to have a regular conversation with Clint Barrows.

"I heard something about the notorious Jeremiah and Jason," she said. "They're giving you trouble."

"*Trouble* is such a kind word." He kept considering his drink until he took another swig, then let out a deep breath, lowering the glass. "See, my grandparents bought this place, turned it into a working ranch, left it to Dad, and he took it from there with Mom. I always had a deep interest in it. They said I was more a cowboy than either of my brothers. Jeremiah and Jason were interested in the money side, and I wasn't. That's the last part I ever cared about."

"You were all about the cutting horses."

"And cattle and ranch hands and everything that goes with the operation. All of us work together to care for, train and breed the cutters."

He seemed proud of what he accomplished on a daily basis. She'd never noticed that about him.

"We've got one hundred and eighty acres of roads and trails, pastures, horse barns, cattle pens, an arena… and all my brothers want to do is start selling off the land to some ag business that will pay top dollar, in spite of the economy. I say that sounds a mite suspicious, if you ask me."

"You don't trust your brothers to have your best interests in mind?"

He seemed to process that. "I'd like to think so. But

brothers don't threaten each other with lawsuits and strong-arming. At least, not the brothers I know."

He was talking about Phi Rho Mu, but she wanted to know more about his blood brothers—whether they were true family or not. "It sounds like Jeremiah and Jason don't care about what you've always done here."

"You're right. When my parents sent them off to college, they became 'businessmen,' and they only see bottom lines. They've always been of one mind, though. Twins."

"I see." She paused. "It almost sounds like they've left you out of their plans."

"That's not the only thing."

She almost asked what he meant, but the moment passed. It almost seemed he got no support around here.... He was on his own.

Margot crossed one booted leg over the other, barely recognizing that she'd turned her body toward him. "From the way you talk, it sounds like your brothers came out of school with a different philosophy than your parents had. What about you?"

He chuckled. "To this day I maintain that I didn't need schooling, but Dad insisted. Mom, though? She said I was a natural for the ranch, no matter how many courses in ag business I took."

"Your brothers disagree, I take it."

"True."

As he leaned his arms on his thighs, he moved into a patch of light. She hadn't ever thought Clint Barrows was capable of a conversation, much less one about business. She wouldn't have guessed he could be serious about anything.

"You've got some brains, stud," she said, lightening the moment. "Who knew?"

He grinned.

"You're the one with the brains," he said. "What with all your books. That's impressive stuff, Dostoyevsky."

In spite of his kidding, she almost cringed. Yeah, being an out-of-work author was truly an achievement.

For some reason, she found herself talking when, with everyone else, she had shut down. It had to be the St. Germain.

"To tell you the truth," she said, "I don't know about my future books."

"You're getting tired of writing them?"

Wouldn't that be an easy excuse to use? *Yes, the reason I'm not publishing more girl-around-the-world books is because I've gotten over the whole scene.*

She hedged. "I'd just love to go a different direction." With her travelogues. With life.

"Which direction do you want to go?" he asked.

So many questions, so few answers.

He gestured toward the night, with its near silence—so quiet she could actually hear herself think for once.

"Know what you should write a book about?" he said. "The *Sex in the City* girl goes country. It'd be one of those... What do you call it?"

"Fish-out-of-water stories?"

"Exactly. You could do one of those blogs, too. Like a journal."

He'd been teasing her, but...

She liked the idea. If only she liked it more than the books she was already writing.

Still, the more she thought about it...

Nah. "That's actually a marketable idea. For someone else."

"But not you." He put his glass on the armrest and placed his hands behind his head, so nonchalantly that she wondered if she'd said something that had rankled him and he was proving that she couldn't affect him at all. "I don't know why I was thinking that you'd want to stay more than a night out in the boonies."

"I'm staying two nights. Give me some credit."

As she tried to get over the fact that he'd been the first person she'd given any hint to about her career predicament, he got out of his chair, took her shot glass, then his and headed for the door.

"One more before the night ends," he said.

While she waited for him to return, she absorbed the sounds around her: a breeze combing through oak leaves, an owl off in the distance, the beautiful quiet she'd noticed before. So peaceful. So much more comfortable than anything she'd heard in all the out-of-the-ordinary places she'd sought.

He came back with her drink, but instead of sitting, he leaned against a porch pillar, staring into the night.

A fist seemed to be squeezing her heart, stopping it for a moment as she ran a gaze down him. If he'd been any other man, she might've…

Done what? Asked him to come back to her room with her?

She squashed her thoughts by talking. "The most country *I* get is going back to my condo. And it's more suburb than country."

"Chico, right? It's a nice area."

"It's a good place to hang my hat after a trip." But as she said it, she realized that the condo was basically a pit stop, just like all the other houses she'd flitted through in her life. Hell, she'd even switched rooms when she'd stayed in the sorority house, telling everyone that she always went for the best upgrade possible.

And, really, had she ever felt as if she'd been at home

while she traveled to places as far away as the cluttered streets of Bangkok? Or had she always just been a visitor, searching for a place where she belonged?

She was getting warm from her drink…or maybe for another reason altogether as she sat there watching Clint under the porch light, his hair thick enough to make her fingers itch to touch it.

And, damn, she really wanted to touch it right now.

He downed the rest of his liqueur, as if he'd needed one last shot before bed, and went toward the door.

"Sweet dreams," he said, and it wasn't even followed by one of his patented, suggestive stud winks.

All alone now, Margot stayed out in the darkness, wishing he was still here and not having a clue why that was.

AFTER SHE TUMBLED out of bed the next morning, Margot made a beeline for the bathroom down the hall, hoping no one would see her with "morning face." She was an expert at saying goodbye to men before the sun lit the sky and they could clearly see the bags she always got under her eyes when she didn't get a good night's sleep.

It wasn't that the guest room bed hadn't been comfortable or the room cozy. Her mind had just been busy, despite sleeping on a feather mattress among the soothing Southwestern décor that Clint's mom must have introduced and he'd never bothered to change.

If she was right about that, she figured she'd probably have liked his mom. Mrs. Barrows would've been a heck of a lot more comfort-minded than Margot's own mother or dad. They hadn't believed in weighing themselves down with furniture, so they'd always lived with the least amount possible.

After Margot emerged from the bathroom, she went

downstairs to find Dani at the long wooden dining room table with a buffet of eggs, cereal, bacon, English muffins, juice and a coffeepot laid out.

"Did you do all this?" Margot asked.

Dani, who looked almost like a stranger with that new hair and a new sweater-and-skirt outfit, put down her newspaper and beamed up at Margot.

"This is all Clint's doing," she said. "Wouldn't he make a good wife?"

"To someone who needs one." Margot took a cactus-patterned plate and began to load it with food. "Where're the guys?"

"Riley was keen to get to the horse barn and hang out with Clint while he put in his work for the day."

"And how're things with Riley?"

"Fine."

Don't interfere, Margot thought. *Don't...*

But Riley was her friend, too, and she couldn't bite her tongue. "He seemed pretty put out with you yesterday. Or did you not notice?"

"I noticed."

Margot ate standing up. "You sure about that? Because you were doing everything you could to avoid talking with him—barely looking at him during dinner and cleaning up afterward in the kitchen while he went to your room."

"Obviously he wasn't bothered by anything, because he was sleeping like a baby when I got to bed."

Margot paused with an English muffin halfway to her mouth. This didn't sound like Dani, who would've never let Riley go to bed angry.

"Is everything okay?" Margot asked.

"Perfect."

"I'm asking because… Frankly, Dani, yesterday was like a day on Mars with you."

Dani neatly folded the newspaper.

"What I mean," Margot said, "is that it seemed like Riley didn't even have a hint that you wanted to quit your job before you announced it. You don't spring things on him like that."

"You're right. He didn't know." Finally, Dani came back to her old self. It was as if she'd never gotten her hair cut or wasn't wearing a sleek sweater that seemed as if it could've been pulled from Margot's closet.

Now Margot did sit. "I understand about cold feet. Your parents weren't exactly good role models for a long-lasting marriage."

Dani sighed. "This has nothing to do with them or with cold feet."

"Okay. But I have to say that it's like something's exploded in you." She motioned toward Dani's bob. "You never, ever changed your hair this drastically before, not in all the years I've known you."

"And that's why I did it." Dani casually stood. "I never have adventures or impulsive moments like you, and I don't have a fabulous new cooking show like Leigh, even though we were both in home ec and we're both just as good in the kitchen. If you want me to be completely honest, seeing where you guys are and where I am really made me reevaluate myself last weekend."

Margot wanted to smack herself. She didn't say it, but she had the feeling that this had a lot to do with her and Leigh and the auction. They'd treated Dani like she couldn't fend for herself.

Worse yet, Margot wondered if this *did* have anything to do with Dani's parents. She didn't know much about psychology, but Dani had always been the wounded bird of the group, torn apart by her mom and dad's separation.

Was it all playing out now?

"Dan," Margot said, going to her, taking her hands in her own. "Do you know that I was wildly envious of your hair, especially back in college when I didn't know what to do with my own mop? Did you know that you always created a menu on dinner nights that made me wish I had even an iota of the talent you have?"

"Please," she said. "You don't have to make me feel better."

"I'm just telling you the truth."

"And I'm telling *you* the truth when I say that…"

She trailed off.

"What, Dani?"

She took her hands from Margot's. "I watch you and Clint. There's chemistry—don't deny it. And I wonder why the room doesn't catch on fire with me and Riley like it does with the two of you."

Margot flinched. "Clint and I don't even like each other."

"Yes, you do. God, you two are hilarious, barely even acknowledging each other when anyone else is around. I mean, really, Margot, nipple tassels and bubble bath?"

She was going to kill Leigh for blabbing.

Dani rolled her eyes. "Just for the record, you guys don't have to stay away from each other's rooms this weekend just because you think Riley and I are idiots."

Well, there it was. Called out.

Margot waited for the world to fall down around her, now that someone had announced the very idea that she'd given in to Clint. But…

The world was still there.

It was everything *inside* her that was crumbling, and that sensation didn't necessarily involve Clint, just book contracts and sales and... Oh, a little thing Margot liked to call an ego.

Dani's gray gaze sparkled now that she'd been successful in changing the subject from her to Margot. "There isn't any chance that you and Clint can..."

"No."

"I wasn't about to say that you should jump all over each other in a bubble bath again. I meant—"

"Definitely no."

Just the thought of trying to wrangle a stud like Clint into what Dani was referring to—a relationship, of all things—was laugh-inducing.

Yet, oddly, Margot didn't feel like laughing.

Taken aback by that, she focused on Dani again. "I hope you and Riley work this out. You're my favorite couple ever, you know."

"Of course we will."

"Because," Margot said, "if anyone in this world would make me want to settle down, it would be a guy like him."

Damn, that sounded pathetic. Not wanting to settle down. She'd been indepen— *No.* It went beyond independence. She'd been lonely for most of her life, and she'd started to lose hope, sticking to the patterns that'd been ingrained in her, moving on, moving on, never planting herself in one spot.

And she was tired. Suddenly so tired of it.

Dani was looking at her as if she knew this conversation was about more than her and Riley.

"I know Riley's a keeper," she said, "and I'm never letting him go."

They hugged, but Margot's own words were the ones

that kept ringing through her mind as an image of Clint Barrows floated over her gaze.

If anyone in this world would make me want to settle down...

As she hugged Dani tighter, Margot told herself that there were more appropriate men to settle down with, even if Clint was the one on her mind and in every cell of her body every second, every minute of the day.

9

THAT EVENING, LONG after Clint and Riley had finished putting in a day's work with the horses and the women had wandered the property to inspect every wedding nook and cranny, Clint settled into the kitchen.

He'd decided to whip up a simple dinner, since Riley had been determined to sit Dani down and have a long talk about what was really going on with her.

He was just putting the main dish in the oven when he heard someone come in the front door.

Margot. It was the way her fashionable boots hit the floor with that easy, swaying stride. Or it could've been wishful thinking.

But he was right, and when she strolled into the kitchen, she greeted him while setting her computer pad down on the table.

"Whatever it is you're cooking smells amazing," she said.

"Lemon-garlic chicken."

"Oh." She laughed. "Good thing Riley is having that up-close-and-personal chat with Dani now and not later."

The garlic. He got it.

"Where did they end up?" he asked.

"The gazebo, I think. Who knows how long they'll be, though."

"Dinner won't be ready for about forty-five minutes, but they can grab some when they're ready."

"You should've asked for help." Margot hovered by his side at the stove, all summer-wind shampoo and skin-fresh heat. "I'm not the world's greatest cook, but I can be of some use."

"It's all under control." He was talking about the food, because *he* sure wasn't anywhere near control. His body felt as if it had a legion of pistons pumping inside him, even though he had nowhere to zoom off to.

Margot gathered some used bowls, transferring them to the sink. She had pulled her dark hair back in a barrette today, and it made the beauty of her face stand out that much more—the high cheekbones, the pale eyes, the feeling that, in spite of her steel spine, she was still a porcelain figurine, delicate and off-limits in so many ways.

As lust—because it was lust, wasn't it?—swirled inside him, she seemed totally unaware of how she threw him into utter inner chaos.

Not knowing what else to do with himself, Clint got out two wineglasses, then a bottle of chilled chardonnay from the fridge. He poured them each a dose.

"Here's to your crazy cooking skills, then," she said as they clinked glasses.

They remained standing by the stove, drinking.

Why was this feeling like a date of sorts?

He could answer that more easily than anything else about them. Dinner was heating up in the oven and they were alone in a house that was silent except for the beat of the grandfather clock in the hallway and the night sounds outside the windows.

Maybe the same date question had entered her mind, too, because she took another belt of wine, as if she needed a buzz to be around him on a personal level.

Click, click, went the clock, chipping away at him.

Finally, he couldn't stand the tension anymore.

They both started to talk at once, then laughed, and he gestured toward her.

"You first." *Please.*

She traced a finger over the ceramic tile of the counter. "I was just going to say that you're full of surprises. Handy with dinner, a house that's way neater and cozier than I anticipated…"

"What did you expect—a cave with a fire for roasting the meat I hunt down every day?"

"That's not too far off the mark."

"Thanks."

"No, I didn't mean for my initial compliment to come out that way." She set her wine on the counter. "It's just that I thought your house would be…"

"The ultimate bachelor pad? Nah. Believe it or not, my dad was a neat freak, an army man before my grandpa passed away and left him this ranch. My brothers and I grew up doing hospital corners on the beds and passing muster every Sunday night to get allowance. Dad was fun-loving, though. He and Mom brought that out in each other."

Margot was watching him closely, a warmth in her gaze, and she seemed to realize it just as he did.

Or had he been mistaken?

Did he even *want* a warmth to be there?

Clint gazed around the kitchen. "Anyway, it just feels

downright disrespectful to not look after what Mom left here after she passed on."

"I'm sorry to hear that—about losing her, I mean."

"It happened a long time ago. I was only old enough to remember that she was here one day and not here the next. She was driving and they say her tire blew out."

"Oh, God, that's awful."

It really had been and, as he looked over the pine-cone clock, the hutch with the desert-patterned plates and the cookie jar with two ceramic bear cubs climbing up the side, he wished she could've been here to see how everything had turned out. How *he* had turned out, loving the home she had loved.

"Dad was the one who kept things as she'd had them," he said. "And when he willed me the house and the ranch, it didn't feel right or necessary to change much. Just a few things here and there."

Even if life had been changing outside the ranch, he'd retained what was familiar and comfortable.

"She had nice taste," Margot said.

"I hate to think of what my brothers might've done with the house. They're both married, so their wives would've probably redecorated." Clint set down his glass. Wine wasn't really his thing, anyway. "Dad invested in a lot of property out of state, and that's where they live, because that's mostly what he left them. But if you look at my share of the ranch, compared with what my brothers inherited, you'd think I came out on the short end."

"You didn't."

"Not by a long shot."

She tilted her head, considering him. "If I didn't know better, I'd say that you've got a nest that you don't care to venture from."

It could be that he did, and hearing Margot say it made him wonder just what her place in Chico looked like.

"I read a couple of your books, you know," he said.

"You did?"

She flushed, and he quelled the sudden, emphatic blip of pleasure in his chest.

"Yeah," he said. "And that's saying something, since I'm not really a bookworm. But I got the impression that you're a restless traveler, not so much someone who feels at home in all the places you visit. You might rather just stay home."

Now she looked pissed. *Well done, stud.*

"That's not true," she said. "Home is nice, but it doesn't…" She swallowed, shrugged. "Challenge me."

Did she believe what she was saying? It didn't seem like it.

It seemed that maybe Margot had been looking for a home for a long time, and she hadn't had one since her sorority days.

"You need a challenge," he said, testing her.

"Don't we all?"

It was like a dare that dangled right in front of him. Why was it that she was the only one who made him want to step out of his comfort zone, even for an hour or two?

But the mere thought of going out into Margot's world discomfited him. He wouldn't ever fit, just like she would never fit into his.

And that's why what they'd had last weekend had suited him fine.

He gave her a challenging look right back, and she raised her chin a bit.

"How did you get to be such a traveler, anyway?" he asked.

"It's in my blood." She got quiet a moment before going on. "I was the only child of parents who had raging cases of wanderlust. I think I've lived in every state of the union. We'd travel out of country, too, when they got the bug."

"Where are they now?"

She smiled a little, sadly. "Long gone. When I was away at Cal-U, they moved into this crummy casita in a bad part of San Diego. But it was exotic, you know? In a colorful, arty section of town. One night, the place had a gas leak."

"Wow. I'm sorry."

"You'd understand how awful it was, as a fellow orphan."

She'd tried to make the conversation lighter, but when the mood didn't lift, she wandered away from the oven, out of the kitchen. He followed, leaving his wine behind.

"So what do you do for excitement around here, anyway?" she asked, pausing at the entrance to the family room. "Watch TV? Tip cows?"

It was an obvious change of subject, and he went with it. "Some nights I'll hang around the hands who stay on the ranch and shoot the breeze with them. Some nights, there's a bar we like to go to, but it's the same people all the time."

"Don't tell me… You get bored of the same chicks over and over again."

"What, you think I've gone through every single woman in the area?"

"I didn't say that."

He leaned against the wall on the opposite side of the door frame. "Ouch. You're hard on me, Dickens."

"That's the price you pay when you're a stud."

Silence. Tension.

Awkward.

He was sick of walking on eggshells, though, so he came right out with what they'd been tiptoeing over all weekend.

"There's one thing I want to know before you go home," he said, "and that's why you didn't just lie to me about what was in your basket. When I overheard you in the bar at the start of the reunion, you said that if someone you didn't like bought it, you were going to adjust the sexy scenarios you'd made up. You were going to make the dates innocent."

She did a slow blink, as if he'd crossed some social boundary. But then she smiled, almost to herself.

"I could've lied to you," she said. "I could've told you that you were mistaken in what you overheard and that there was nothing sexual in that basket at all. But you wouldn't have let me get away with that."

Getting her to admit that she was attracted to him was a real bitch. But, again, it was a challenge.

And challenges always seemed to work with them.

He lifted an eyebrow. "Le Crazy Horse, Paris. How would you have spun that for someone who didn't know any better?"

"Easy. I would've taken him for a horse ride and fixed a French-food picnic for him while regaling him with tales about my time in the City of Light."

"Not bad. I guess that's why you write for a living."

She got the same sad expression on her face that he'd noticed yesterday, and he wanted to ask her why.

But she had already banished the sentiment, as if by pure will alone.

"Just think," he said, wanting to see her get fired up again. "Brad could've had all eighty ways."

"How about we never bring him up again? From what I heard through the grapevine after the reunion, my ex-boyfriend's back home, chasing around the wife who left him. If I'd known…"

"You didn't. Don't beat yourself up about it."

So no more Brad. He didn't like to think about Margot's initial basket date of choice, anyway.

Clint went into the family room, where he'd stored her basket in a cabinet. He'd thought about displaying it on the fireplace mantel, just to get her goat, but he'd decided against it after they'd somewhat called this truce or whatever it was between them.

But, now, he couldn't resist.

When he took it out of the cabinet, she groaned.

"Don't get uppity," he said, pulling out a slip of paper. "I just want to hear you in action. Besides, I didn't get to claim more than one scenario."

"We just had one night, remember? Besides, I wasn't in the mood." She swirled her wine in its glass. "But then again, why not? It's better than TV."

Somewhat surprised that she'd agreed to go forward, he read the destination.

"This one says *'Kama Sutra.'* How would you have explained that?"

She sat on the cowhide sofa. "It would've been trickier than Le Crazy Horse."

"The *Kama Sutra* is a sex book, right?"

"Yes, but it's also a guide to gracious and virtuous living. It talks about family and love, too, and how to take delight out of all aspects of life. I would've prepared some Indian food, talked about deep philosophical stuff with my date and maybe have given him a chaste, yet soulful kiss at the end of the evening."

He chose another slip of paper. "'Lupanar, Pompeii.'"

She sank back into the cushions. "That's one of my favorites. Italy's the best, especially the Roman ruins."

"Pompeii is where that volcano erupted. But I have no idea what a lupanar is."

"Well, I could've spun that one as the literal translation for lupanar—a 'den of she-wolves.' I could've centered that basket date on an evening in the woods with a dinner that had lots of sloppy meat and finger foods."

"But what's the real definition of the term?"

Margot flashed him a sassy grin. "A brothel. The most famous one in Pompeii. You can still view the erotic paintings on the walls."

He tucked the paper into his jeans pocket. He could already imagine what Margot would've done with this one if he had picked it last weekend.

"The Lupanar isn't a terribly romantic place," she said. "It had about ten rooms because it was a bigger brothel than most in Pompeii. Wealthy people didn't really visit those places, either, because they had mistresses or slave concubines. And the beds? They were mattresses on brick platforms. It was the paintings that interested me."

She smoothed a stray, dark lock of hair back over her shoulder, a sensual move that dug deep into Clint. Then she set her wine on an end table, relaxing back into the cushions.

Talking about the basket had done something to her, and Clint realized that everything she had written down was as much a fantasy for her as it was for him.

She watched him, and he watched her.

"What're we going to do about this?" he finally asked.

"I really have no idea."

But he had one, and it involved turning off the oven in the kitchen and turning on Margot in the bedroom while Riley and Dani were still out of the house.

WHY AM I DOING THIS? Margot kept asking herself. She'd assuaged her curiosity about Clint already, but here she was, following him out of the living room.

This would never go anywhere. Forget the video incident—that was in the past. But the closer he got to her, the more she realized that she had no idea how to relate to anyone on a profound level. Her parents sure hadn't given her much insight into being loved, and they had made her feel that it was necessary to never get deep, to always keep a buffer between her and someone else because she wouldn't be around for much longer, moving on, moving on…

Just the old, tried-and-true sex. That's what she needed.

That's what she wanted.

And she was about to get it here in Clint's room, she thought, as he shut and locked the door behind them.

"Tell me about one of those paintings in the Lupanar, Margot," he said softly, and even from across the room, his voice had the power to send goose bumps over her flesh.

She went to his large bed, running a hand over the iron footboard. Was this really her, in a lion's den instead of one that belonged to she-wolves?

Yep. And she was going to enjoy this for what it was, nothing more.

"There are a lot of paintings that feature the phallus,"

she said to start off. "*Huge* ones. You wouldn't believe the size of those penises."

Behind her, she heard the rustle of clothing, and her body flashed with heat.

Lust. It was just lust.

She didn't turn around yet. Allowing her pleasure to also be pain, she reveled in the craving to see him in the flesh again, without that shirt, without those jeans, tanned and bare and rippling with hard-labor muscles.

She kept talking. "There's also graffiti on the walls. *Hic ego puellas multas futui.* I remember that one. The loose translation of the Latin is 'Here I screwed many girls.'"

Had she meant that to be a dig at Clint's college lifestyle?

"Sounds charming," he said.

He was closer now, but she didn't turn around. Not when there were a thousand delicious tingles running down her spine.

"There's another painting that I remember well," she murmured. "Two naked people on a bed. The man has the woman's legs over his lap, but there's a space between them."

He was right behind her now, and she kept remembering the day he had touched her from behind, massaging her into a climax that had rolled through her with a ferocious growl.

"Take off your clothes, Margot."

Her name sounded just as bare as he probably was, but she found herself obeying him. It would be the last time, though.

Just one more time.

She peeled off her sweater, skirt, boots…everything.

Then she went to the bed on her own before he could demand anything else of her.

Bold as you please, she slid onto the quilt, her back against the pillows that bunched at the headboard. She kept her knees together, refusing to show him more than she wanted to right now.

But the sight of *him* rocked her—broad shoulders, chest. Those abs.

And his cock.

It was ready for her as he climbed onto the bed and brought her legs over his lap.

"Did that painting look something like this?" he asked.

"Yes."

He swept his fingertips up her leg, coming down the side of it. Her nipples went stiff, her center dampening.

Such an intimate touch, she thought, her heartbeat quickening, telling her it was time to run.

But she was staying for some reason.

Her body, she thought. This was what she needed from him tonight.

As he circled his fingers over her belly, making her shift, butterflies clustered inside of her, swiping her with light flutters that winged up to her chest, around her heart.

She chased them off. "There's another picture I remember. On a bed again, a woman riding a man."

His smile was tight, as if he knew that she couldn't take the intimacy. Maybe he couldn't, either.

He guided her into position—her on top, him on the bottom, his hands braced on her hips.

Giving him a look, lashes lowered, she imitated the painting further, putting her hand on his head.

"The woman in the painting was doing this. I think

it was because she wanted to show him that she was in charge."

"She wouldn't have it any other way."

His words went beyond a comment on the painting, straight to a reflection of her, but he didn't elaborate, instead reaching toward a nightstand into a drawer. He came out with a condom and tore into the packaging.

She took it from him, then slowly covered his cock.

"Was the man's 'phallus' inside the woman in that painting?" Clint asked, teasing, referencing those penis pictures she had mentioned while a pulse throbbed in his neck.

"You can't really tell, but I'm assuming so."

With that, she impaled herself on him, already slick with desire.

He went so deeply into her that she moaned, then began moving her hips, making him go in, out.

She'd already removed her hand from his head, but just so he wouldn't forget that this was still a painted fantasy and nothing more, she started to put it back in position.

He intercepted her before she could recreate the picture, instead placing her hand over his chest.

His heart.

A tiny explosion went off inside her, and it wasn't centered in her belly this time. It was higher, in a place that was usually so still.

Even so, she didn't take her hand away from him. She left it there, feeling the beat of his heart—*bang, bang, bang.* Feeling him inside her, a part of her, thick and long and perfect.

That last thought jarred her.

Perfect?

It was too much for her, and she switched position, turning around so he couldn't see her face.

He made a throttled sound as she rode him backward while he held her hips, pulling her back to him, pushing her forward.

She bent so that her hands were on his legs, so that she could get to an orgasm before…

Before what? Before she lost part of herself to a man who would probably only end up hurting her even worse than he'd done years ago?

He came with a curse-laden blast, then another, but she still labored, strained, a fierce and brutal pressure clicking inside of her like the clock downstairs, counting down.

One click—almost there…

Two—coming…

Three…four…*five*…

A pounding climax struck, making her vibrate in every cell until she lost all strength, slumping down on him.

But instead of leaving her like that, he pulled her back to him, tugging the covers around them and possessing her within the cradle of his arms.

Warm.

Intimate.

As she lay against his chest, she let herself become a part of him, her skin against his, melding together. She pictured nights when she wouldn't want to go anywhere, when she would only want to listen to the sounds outside, or the creaks of this old house speaking to her with reassuring welcome.

And, for a moment, it seemed so real. So possible.

But then the adrenaline started to thread through

her as she pictured him, going to another woman…or
another place, leaving her behind for something better.

She pushed the images away until they faded to almost nothing, just like an old painting.

HE PLAYED WITH her hair, just as he'd always wanted to
do. Margot wasn't even objecting, and that shocked the
hell out of him.

What'd just happened?

In the midst of his afterglow fog, Clint wasn't sure,
but he'd never experienced anything like it in his life.
There'd been a closeness he hadn't expected, though
now, in the aftermath, he could admit that he'd wanted
it more than anything.

Too bad it'd happened with a woman who didn't want
anything more from him than re-creations of brothel
paintings.

"You awake?" he asked. Through the window, he
could see it was dark. Bedtime.

"Yeah," she said.

He didn't know what he wanted from *her* exactly—
the sense that she felt more for him than she should?
The hope that she might stick around a little longer?

After blowing out a here-goes-nothing breath, he
said, "That night in college…I didn't bring you up to
my room just to make out with you, you know."

She waited for him to continue, almost as if she
didn't want him to.

He rushed ahead. "I actually wanted to…." God, this
wasn't easy. "I guess I wanted to see what you really
thought of that movie."

She stirred, her hair brushing against his skin.

He said, "So that's why I brought you there."

"What I'm hearing in man-speak," she said, "is that

you wanted to get to know me, and the making-out part was incidental?"

Why had he even brought this up? The things a man said after he'd come. Jeez.

She seemed to realize his sudden discomfort, and tentatively draped an arm over his torso.

"I'm glad you told me that."

"Why?"

She swallowed. "Because it makes me feel… Just thank you. And, by the way, Riley told me that you made sure no one bothered me about the video when we were at the reunion. Thank you for that, too. It was thoughtful."

There was more to what she was saying. He knew it.

She smoothed her fingers down his ribs. "I had a little crush on you back then. There was good reason you attracted so many women."

"And you were curious about more than just my charm?"

"Very. But I was also wary, and it took everything I had to go up to that room. And when I saw that camera…"

"You still blame me for that?" He caressed her arm.

"No. But at that point, I thought you just wanted to nail me for bragging rights, especially afterward, when that tape popped up everywhere." She slid her hand under him, her breasts crushed to his chest. "Before I saw the camera, though, I thought there was something…"

Sounded like the truth bug had her tongue, too.

"What if there was something?" he asked.

She looked up at him, her hair falling over half her face, and he could feel the bad news coming.

"Clint," she whispered. "I really do like being with you."

Although she had completely avoided answering him, she couldn't have been any clearer if she'd hit him over the head with a rock.

But when she drew her leg on top of his thighs, nestling against his hip, nuzzling him beneath his jaw, he wondered if what they had together was clear to *her*.

10

OUTSIDE, THE NIGHT was mild, but the distance between Dani and Riley as they sat face-to-face on the benches in the gazebo was as chilly as it could get.

Moonlight filtered in through the open walls, shading Riley slightly. Over his shoulder, Dani could see the outline of bunkhouses in the near distance, and even the tip of the horse barn farther down the hill. Country music was playing, probably coming from a ranch hand's room.

Actually, Merle Haggard had been the only sound between Dani and Riley for the past few minutes, and she was just about ready to burst.

"You're still mad at me," she finally said.

"Not mad." Riley was staring off into the distance, his hair darker in the moonlight. "I'm just confused. Lately, it's like I don't recognize you at all."

She knew he wasn't talking about the new hairstyle or clothing, either. They were stuck on this whole thing about her wanting to quit her job.

"I've told you why I want to try something on my own," she said. "We're going to have a lot more money in our savings account since Clint is letting us have the ranch for the wedding. And I found a reasonably priced gown all on my own. It's vintage. Someone's selling it on eBay, and that'll save us money, too—"

"I'm not talking about our wedding." He exhaled. "Do you remember everything we've worked for during the past few years? We've planned and plotted how to get ourselves out of that rental house, for starters."

"We can still do that." Eventually. "I like where we're living, Riley. You're the one who wants to move out, right?"

"That's because I thought we'd be further along than we are these days." His posture was stiff, as if his pride was the one thing holding him upright. "I never wanted to run small estates, and someday, there's going to be a bigger one with bigger perks."

"You already give me what I need," she said. "Those dreams of a big wedding were just girlish fantasies. I'm happier with you than I could ever dream of being with anyone else. Can't you see that?"

So was that why she was cutting her hair and quitting her job and having an early-life crisis?

Her heart reached out to Riley, the best man she would ever find. He was her one, her only, and she was making a mess of what they had.

She didn't mean to, though.

So why was it happening?

Scooting over on the bench, closer to him, she tugged on his shirtsleeve, toying with it. "I think I'm going about this all wrong."

"I just wish I knew what you were going *about*."

She paused. Should she lay it all out in front of him? What if he didn't understand?

The words barely got out of her, then they began

tumbling like an avalanche she'd been trying to keep back. "I've been asking myself so many questions.... But, well, the biggest ones have to do with making all the right choices. How do I know that I'm not losing opportunities left and right because I haven't opened myself to them?" She inched even nearer to Riley, smelling his barely there, clean cologne. It filled her in so many ways. "But there is one thing I know for sure, and it's that you're the right decision. That's never going to change."

He held her hand, their fingers entwining.

In the near distance, Merle Haggard sang his outlaw country songs. Riley seemed content just to touch Dani, so she enjoyed the feel of his fingers wrapping around hers, safe, warm, like a cocoon.

But even cocoons needed to open at some point and reveal the changes that had taken place inside. And that was the true issue here, wasn't it?

It didn't necessarily make sense to her, but there it was.

Why did she feel so restless these days? And why was it happening even now, as the music infiltrated her, making her heartbeat speed up as she ran her thumb along Riley's?

Did he have any idea what was underneath the layers she wore? And she meant that literally, because she had hoped that they would be talking tonight, alone. She had hoped that, at some point, they would be stripping the layers off, one by one.

She moved closer to him. "Is everything good with us?"

"Everything's good."

He was looking down at their joined hands, his heart in every word he said.

Her Riley. Her good guy in a figurative white hat.

"Time to make up, then?" she asked on a whisper.

"We always do."

She didn't know what got into her exactly, but she crossed one leg over the other flirtatiously. He caught the gesture and lifted an eyebrow.

"Do you realize," she asked, "that we've never had make-up sex before?"

"That's because this was our first real fight, even after all these years."

Yeah, two even-keeled, levelheaded people. That was them. The first time they'd been together, he had pulled out all the romantic stops—the roses, the champagne, the *I Love Yous*. Nothing had gone wrong that night.

And nothing had since then, except for lately.

She subtly unbuttoned the tight sweater she'd purchased just this week—something that made her feel sexier than usual.

Even in the low light, she saw Riley's gaze go steamy. "Dani…"

She smiled, feeling like a little devil. Reveling in the urgency that had been creeping up on her this past week.

"This is our first time really fighting," she said. "I like that you care enough for me to get angry."

Again, he looked at her as if he'd never seen her before, but there was also an unknown quality in his eyes that drove her on, making her undo her sweater even more.

She couldn't wait to show him what she had under the layers, what she'd planned for their make-up time.

"We should go back to the room," he said.

"No."

He had started to get to his feet, but she pulled him

back down and began to work at her sweater buttons again.

When she was done, Riley's eyes were wide.

She had parted her sweater to show him the bra she'd purchased on the sly at The Boudoir before they'd left Avila Grande last weekend. It was a creation she'd *never* thought of buying before, and doing so had been an act of freedom.

Bras like this were for other girls.

But not anymore.

Dani could feel him running his gaze over her breasts, which were exposed, thanks to the nonexistent cups and black half-corset underneath.

As he stared, her nipples went hard. "You should see my undies and the garter belt with stockings."

Crotchless. She'd bought a set.

"Out here?" His voice was gritty. "What if one of the ranch hands walks by? What if Clint does?"

"We'll be really quiet. And it's dark enough in this gazebo so that we can just hold our breath and wait for them to pass by." She leaned toward him. "Come on, Riley. Make up with me."

This time, he stood all the way before she could pull him back down.

He began to scoop her into his arms. "We're going to the room."

"No," she said, pulling her sweater down her shoulders to her arms so he could see that she wasn't backing down, then gaining her feet and stepping away from him.

If he'd been bewildered by her before, he looked totally dumbfounded now.

Dani reached for his belt buckle. "Let's do it out here."

"On a bench?"

Wow. She wasn't sure they were ever going to have make-up sex at this rate.

"Yes, on a bench," she said. "Other people have done it in stranger places. The most exotic we've ever gotten was in your truck once."

"Maybe I'll order up some kinky equipment for a dungeon when we get back home," he said, sarcasm lacing his voice.

She'd stung him, had basically called their sex vanilla.

But making love with him had always been fulfilling. She just wanted…

More?

But what *kind* of more?

A thought sliced into her: was she pushing him away before it could happen years on down the road?

No. That wasn't it at all.

Shoving aside those thoughts, she sought out physical answers, guiding Riley firmly to that bench, bowling him over.

He grumbled her name, giving in as her breasts spilled out of that half-corset.

As he kissed her fervently, cupping her, circling her nipples and making her squirm on his lap, she thought she heard the music from the bunkhouses cut off, leaving only the memory of notes in her head.

But it was the present that mattered, because this was what she wanted from Riley—recklessness, passion, the wildness of doing it anywhere they wanted just because they could.

Did good girls like the old Dani have sex in the open like this? Nope. Did goody-goody home ec majors who had a perfect home life wear wicked bras and undies with slits in the crotch?

Now they did.

Just as Riley was unzipping her skirt, she heard a shout from near the bunkhouses, and he abruptly stopped kissing her, closing her sweater.

Was it a ranch hand who'd come out for a ramble around the property and a smoke?

"Dammit," he said. "No arguments now, Dani. I'm getting you out of here."

"Riley." She put all her weight on him, emphasizing that she didn't want to go anywhere.

Her pulse was running too hard, her belly too knotted with desire. She wanted Riley to want it as much as she did.

As another shout in the distance turned into laughter, she realized that some of the ranch hands were probably yipping it up outside their quarters, drinking beer, socializing. Their laughter floated on the night, making it seem as if they were closer than they really were.

"Let's do it," she said, pulling at his shirt. "Who cares if someone sees?"

He looked at her as if he *really* didn't recognize her now, and she knew what he had to be asking himself.

Despite what she'd told him, *did* she want more from this relationship than they had?

Carefully, he began to button her sweater, his mouth set in a grim line.

He was angry with her again.

"The girl I used to know," Riley said, "would've had more pride in herself than that."

He took her by the hips, setting her on her feet.

Her body still thudding with need, she turned on her

heel, leaving the gazebo. She wasn't sure if it was because she was mad at him, or if she was just mortified.

"Dani!" he shouted.

But *she* wasn't even sure she recognized herself by name.

MARGOT WAS UP much earlier than usual the next morning.

She'd crept out of Clint's bed just as soon as the sun had eased through his curtains. Thinking that she ought to be in her room before Riley and Dani discovered otherwise, she'd made her way over the floorboards to her discarded clothing. Then, after she was dressed, she was out his door.

Just her luck, though—Riley was already up.

And he was coming out of what she thought had been an unused guest room.

She froze when he saw her, then decided that there was no way out of this one.

"You got me," she whispered in an oh-well tone.

Riley grinned at her, but there was a melancholy slant to it.

She'd joined him downstairs in the kitchen, and while they waited for their coffee to brew, Riley spilled his heart out to her about Dani.

Now, an hour later, Margot had just gone into the bathroom to take a shower when a light knock sounded on the door. It was Dani. "We're leaving," she said, obviously having showered in another bathroom.

Her hair was neatly styled and she wore a trace of lightly applied makeup, but Dani was out of sorts, with bags under her eyes.

"Oh, Dani." Margot hugged her friend. Riley had

made it sound as if he didn't know what to do with her, but she wished she knew Dani's side of the story.

"Will you call me if you need to talk?" she asked, holding Dani at arm's length so she could meet her gaze. "Anytime, anywhere. Okay?"

"You know I will. But Riley and I will be fine." Dani swallowed. "We always are."

They said goodbye, and Margot watched her go down the stairs, wondering what the ride home for them would be like.

As she shut the door again, she plugged in the hair-dryer, drowning out everything else. Worry weighed on her, and not just because of Dani.

She'd been trying not to think about Clint, too.

Things had gone so far beyond a basket-bound thing that she wasn't sure where she stood with him.

Maybe it didn't even matter, because she was leaving soon, anyway. No more Stud Barrows. No more...

She shut off the dryer. No more whatever it was that had turned her into a mental case.

Reaching for her makeup bag, she heard the floor creak outside the bathroom.

"Dani?"

Was she back, putting off the ride home in favor of having a heartfelt talk with a girlfriend?

But when Margot opened the door, it wasn't Dani standing there.

"Crap," she muttered, thinking of closing the door so he couldn't see her bare morning face.

But then she thought better of that. Oddly, he didn't seem to notice her lack of makeup.

"You disappeared early," he said, leaning against the door frame. She wondered if that was his position of choice, just like Robert Redford would've done in that cowboy movie he was in back when he was young and golden.

She dabbed some creamy foundation on her face, pretending that Clint had seen her primp a thousand times before.

This was just another show for him. Le Crazy Au Natural.

"I wasn't tired anymore," she said. "Besides, getting up at the crack of dawn gave me the chance to talk with Riley."

"Yeah. Before he left, he mentioned what's going on with Dani."

"Do you think their truck will freeze over before they get home?"

"I think they'll be okay. They're Dani and Riley."

She slid him a glance. They *had* been Dani and Riley before the reunion.

With purposeful efficiency, Margot uncapped her mineral powder and extracted the large powder brush from her bag. He was watching her every move, as if fascinated.

"I've been thinking," he said.

"Danger ahead."

"Seriously, Margot." He reached toward the counter, grabbing a tube of crimson lipstick, opening the top and spinning it until the red emerged. "What if you stayed here in the country for a couple more days, just to see if there really is a book in this for you?"

"The *Sex in the City* fish-out-of-water idea?" She finished dusting powder over her face, then took her lipstick from him. "I told you that I didn't think it was for me."

"How can you be sure about that?"

He had a question for everything.

But she made him wait for her answer as she applied the red to her lips.

When she was done, he looked at her mouth as if he had been having a few lipstick fantasies.

Desire cascaded over her, but she continued with her makeup application, fetching her blush.

Was he proposing that she stay here for a short time because he was interested in the well-being of her career? Or was it because he wanted more basket time?

A few days ago, she would've guessed the latter. But he'd shown a genuine curiosity in her writing. He'd read some of her books, which still stunned the tar out of her.

And they'd had that intimacy last night, complete with a conversation that neither one of them had been able to fully articulate their way through.

"I was going to go home and start research for my next project," she said. But she recognized the pattern.

Distance.

Time to go?

"Just do your research here," he said.

Well, it wasn't as if she was doing anything else since her contracted book had been canceled. Besides, he really did have a pretty good idea.

Should she do it?

Yes.

She answered before her instincts could overwhelm her, trap her just as they'd always done.

"Okay." She put down her blusher and went for her eye shadow. "Why the hell not?"

There were a million reasons.

"Good," Clint said, not going anywhere. "I already have plans for tonight."

"You do?"

"I'm going to ease you back into small-town life. You

might have gone to a college with a lot of cowboys in it, but Avila Grande's bars aren't real country."

He reached into the bathroom again, taking hold of her makeup bag and bringing out her mascara. With one of those arrogant grins, he handed the tube to her, as if he'd become a part of her daily routine.

But Margot made herself a promise: even if she was staying here a little longer, it didn't mean he was a part of a daily or nightly anything for her.

Or ever would be.

CLINT'S FAVORITE LOCAL bar was called The 76, named after the old, abandoned Phillips 76 gas station garage that it had taken up residence in.

He parked among the other trucks in front of the closed, rusted pumps, then went around to Margot's side to open her door.

A loud Kenny Chesney tune boomed through the open metal doors of the large converted garage.

Clint reached for Margot, taking her by the hand to help her down. She needed the help, too, since she was wearing a pair of black, high-heeled, city-street boots that came up to her knees. And he knew he was going to have to keep an eye out for her when the cowboys inside got a load of her in that tight burgundy, long-sleeved dress.

She'd also pinned her hair away from her face, leaving it to fall in a tumble of dark layers down her back, exposing a pair of dangling bronze earrings that she said were lotus blossoms.

"Thank you," she said as he helped her down.

He kept hold of her hand for a moment longer, smelling her flowery perfume. But then she was off like a shot, heading toward the building.

Research, he thought.

Shaking his head, he watched her go, swaying hips, cosmopolitan-girl attitude and all.

Did she have any idea that he was a storm of hormones, just from being around her? Worse yet, did she realize that he couldn't get his mind off her, day or night?

A temporary addiction, he kept repeating to himself as he followed her inside. *That's all this is.*

The place was hopping, even on a Monday night. It was happy hour, after all, and the beers were cheap.

She had stopped just inside, surveying the place: the plank floorboards sprinkled with sawdust, the dance floor, the tire racks on the walls, the air-hockey and foosball tables near the back, manned by a bunch of local ranch hands and farmers in tractor baseball caps.

"Country enough for you?" he asked.

She ran a hand down the side of her dress, as if second-guessing her wardrobe choice. A fish out of water, all right.

"Actually," she said over the music, close to his ear, "it's exhilarating after a day of being holed up in my room with the computer."

Her words had warmed his skin, and it tingled, bathed with her breath.

Off she went to a table near the dance floor, where cowboys and cowgirls were line-dancing.

She took a seat, but not before he noticed that just about every shitkicker in the joint was eyeing her. He gave them a back-off look—even the fellows who worked with him on the ranch.

They laughed, and went back to their beers, knowing that they needed to keep their paws off Clint's "guest."

A few small TVs flashed with the Monday-night

football game, and one of the waitresses, Lula, came to their table.

Big-haired, blonde Lula, with her baby blues and her cut-off mechanic's uniform.

"What can I do you for?" she asked in a thick drawl.

He wished she didn't have such a "Helloo, Clint," look in her eyes. Then again, a few of the waitresses here would be glancing at him that way, seeing as he'd given them something to go *helloo* about a time or two.

What could he say? It was a small town.

"The usual for me," he said. Then he ordered for Margot. "And a Midori Sour."

When Lula had departed, Margot assessed him with those seen-it-all eyes.

"How did you know about the Midori?" she asked.

"You were drinking one the first night of the reunion," he said. "And it was your favorite in college. It's a pretty standout cocktail, being all green and everything."

"Has anyone ever told you that you've got quite a memory on you?"

The music switched to a slow Collin Raye song, and the people on the floor transitioned into a two-step. Clint focused on them.

"My memory's the last thing I depend on," he said. "Trivia doesn't have much use in my business."

Margot leaned forward, and he tried not to fix his attention on her cleavage. He wasn't even sure she meant to seduce him with it right now.

"You know what you should do with your business and your brothers?"

"Should I ask?"

She ignored that. "Get a kick-ass, top-notch lawyer

who'll make them pee their pants when they toss their next threat at you. Or have you already consulted one?"

He hesitated to tell her that he'd merely talked to a local attorney, but he was no bulldog. And Clint had been too proud to give details to any of the Phi Rho Mu brothers who had gone into law, even though rumors about his troubles had been making the rounds.

It was as if Margot read him. "I know someone who could help."

He didn't know what to say. He wasn't used to offers of support.

"You can recommend someone from your travels?" he asked.

"Sort of. But if you're thinking that there's a conflict of interest because I slept with him, you're wrong. He's married to my agent in Los Angeles. He's good, Clint, and if he can't do it, he'll know someone else who deals with ag business."

His emotions turned quickly. It'd been one thing to give Margot details about his brothers, but this was another.

Too personal.

Too much of a slap to that pride of his.

"First you meddled in Dani's wedding," he said in mild retaliation, "and now you're arranging my business? You're a real orchestrator." The fact that he'd arranged for her to stay on at the ranch to do all that research didn't escape him, but he didn't mention it.

She pressed her lips together and sat back in her chair, taking a silverware set rolled in a paper napkin from a small aluminum pail.

Once again you've done it, stud. "Sorry. It's just that this is the last thing I want to talk about right now."

"I understand." She smiled. "It's true that I meddle. I own that about myself."

As she let his comment roll off her like springwater, he decided that she wasn't fibbing. She did own it, and he liked that about her.

But did he have the guts to tell her that her idea had actually been a sound one? That, if circumstances were different, the two of them might have made a good team—him giving her ideas, while she gave him advice?

Lula returned with their drinks, setting them on the table. "Buffalo wings will be up in a jiff, plus those American fries you like."

"Thanks, Lula."

Before she left, she gave Margot the once-over, then strode away.

Margot watched after her, then turned back to Clint.

He shook his head. "Before you say something, the answer's no. I didn't bring you here so you could see Lula using her wiles on me."

"What makes you think I was going to ask that?"

God, he didn't know *why* he'd brought her here, or even why he'd asked her to stay a couple more days. The book idea had been a flimsy excuse, and he knew that she knew it.

He thought of the last time they'd been together, in his bed, him holding her, smelling her hair, trying to absorb every part of her.

It had taken all of his courage to admit that, years ago, he'd gone up to that dim room to meet her because he thought something real could happen between them.

And she'd been forced to admit she'd done the same. But what was he doing with her now?

Trying, he thought. *Hoping.*

That last realization shook him.

He really did want something more with Margot. Deep inside, he'd always thought about the one who'd gotten away, and when he'd had a chance with her again, he'd taken it, not just because of sex, either.

It was because he was tired of floating along, cooking dinner for himself most nights, coming to this bar and seeing the same people over and over and never getting anywhere.

So why was he just sitting here hoping when he could do a hell of a lot more?

He got out of his chair and went over to her side of the table. She was drinking her Midori Sour, and as he stood by her, she put down her cocktail and looked up at him.

Was there something in her gaze?

Something to hope for?

He held out his hand as the two-step kept playing over the sound system.

Biting her lip, she looked at her drink, as if the taste of it was lingering in her mouth, helping her to remember what it'd been like to drink Midori in college, go to the small country bars, dance to the down-home music.

She took his hand, and he smiled.

"I don't remember how to do this," she said as he led her to the dance floor.

"Just let me lead, Margot."

"I…" She stumbled in those high boots. "I don't know how to let anyone lead. I never have."

"Trust me."

He had her dancing in no time, keeping her in a firm grip that was gentle at the same time. He loved the feel of his palm on her waist, her hand in his.

Skin to skin, heartbeat to heartbeat—that "something" he'd been hoping for pounded in the slight space between them.

Since they'd joined in the dance late, the music didn't last long. It trailed off as the DJ invited people to participate in a foosball contest.

Meanwhile, the two of them stayed on the floor, still holding on to each other, even without a song to join them.

Suddenly, they were back in college, on *that* night. But it was as if this were a do-over.

A chance to make things right.

He wanted to kiss her now, needed to, because in spite of all the sex, they hadn't had a moment like this yet. They hadn't had a heart-to-heart kiss full of real emotion and innocence.

They were close, so very close, and they got even closer with every breath.

Two inches apart. One and a half.

A quarter of an inch.

Their lips could've touched if he moved only a fraction more.

But then he heard the crowd around them, and he realized that this was not the place for the intimacy he hungered for.

"Later, Margot," he whispered in her ear. "We're going to take this up with each other later."

He drew away from her, and she looked at him a second longer, as if figuring out what he was all about. Then she laughed softly and headed back to their table.

Did she think he'd been teasing her again, setting her up for another sexual game?

As he returned to the table, too, he told himself that he definitely would find out later, after they got back home.

_11_

AS THE NIGHT went on, Margot just sat there in her seat, tapping her foot to the pumping music and thinking that, sometime, Clint was going to stop nursing the damn beer he'd been working on the entire time and ask her to dance again.

Why did she have the feeling he knew that she was waiting?

And waiting.

Eventually, she decided that she would gainfully occupy herself and show him that she had other things to do.

When the Monday-night football game ended and a band came on stage, encouraging a bunch of cowboys to swing their partners around the floor, Margot got out her phone and began texting with Dani.

How's everything with you and Riley?

A few minutes passed. Then, an answer.

A-OK. Still some things to work out, but hard feelings put aside.

That news lifted Margot's spirits, and by the time the band launched into a song that brought out the line-steppers, she was done with being on the fringes.

"Let's go," she yelled to Clint over the gyrating guitar riff in "Footloose."

He shrugged and sent her one of his cocky grins, as if he'd known all along that she would be the one asking him to dance.

"I'm doing fine right here," he said.

Jerk. But he'd see that two could play at this.

Glancing around the bar, she caught the eye of a tanned, tall cowpoke—a guy she'd seen speaking to Clint earlier when he'd gone to the bar to get Margot another Midori Sour after Lula had inexplicably decided to give them the worst service imaginable.

She smiled at Mr. Tall and Tanned, but after a beat in which she actually thought he might ask her to dance, he looked at Clint, then away from her.

She got the hint loud and clear.

"Did you spread the word that I wasn't available?" she asked.

He finished his beer. "I might've mentioned it."

Oh, really?

Well, screw this. She went to the floor, to a spot not far from their table, and joined a line of dancing cowboys and girls. All night long, she'd been studying how they moved, as well as the different steps, and those college nights when she used to Electric Slide and Tush Push til closing time came back to her with a vengeance.

As she stepped and slid and wiggled her butt more than the dance really called for, she locked gazes with Clint, giving him the same cocky smile he'd sent her earlier.

But now, the expression on his face wasn't so self-satisfied. His mouth was set in a firm line while his hand gripped his empty beer bottle.

Ha! A taste of his own teasing medicine. She hoped he liked it. And she hoped he was regretting that moment earlier in the night when he'd almost kissed her.

She swore that he had come *this* close to doing it, his lips nearing hers until… Well, until the jerk had pulled away from her, playing her for a fool for real this time.

She'd hidden her mortifying frustration well, nonchalantly walking back to their table, but damn him, she'd somehow been anticipating—and worrying about—more than the games they'd been engaging in tonight.

As the song ended, the cowboys around the area applauded her hip-shaking performance. She made a playful show of turning to each and every one of them, thanking them, then facing the table again to gift Clint with a right-back-at-you grin.

But he wasn't there.

And she knew just where he'd gone when she felt a hand on her arm from behind, firmly guiding her through the appreciative crowd and toward the exit.

"Nice show," he said tightly.

"I try my best to entertain."

They were in the parking lot in record time, and he opened the passenger door with such a pull that she thought he might tear it right off.

"Is Alpha Male angry?" she asked.

"Just get in."

A thrill spun inside of her, but after a second, it didn't feel right. A week ago it certainly would have, but now?

Now she wanted to ask him what was wrong, just to see if he would answer truthfully. She wanted him to admit that he might've been a teeny-weenie bit jealous while hearing those other men applaud her line dance.

They drove back to the ranch with the radio on full volume, the tires roaring over the country road until finally they passed under the iron arch that announced the Circle BBB. When they reached the ranch house, Clint snapped off the radio and wasted no time in alighting from the truck.

She opened her own door, thank you, shutting it and following him up the steps.

"I'd call the night a major success," she said. "*Very* good research for that fish-out-of-water book. I might have to go back there tomorrow and drag some of those cowboys onto the dance floor, just to gather more anecdotal color for a possible story."

God help her, but she'd meant to goad Clint—it was a part of that "push them away" deal she had going on. And as he came to the door, he paused.

Goaded, indeed.

Why did she have the feeling that he was about to get serious?

Did she want him to?

A spark of that familiar panic that she got only when she was around Clint popped inside her. No way. She absolutely didn't want him to get serious on her.

Thank goodness he didn't do anything else but open the door, then stand aside to let her in while sweeping off his hat.

"After you, Fitzgerald," he said.

She brushed right by him. "Would you stop calling me those names?"

"They're compliments."

She opened her mouth to retort, but closed it. How could she tell him that every nickname he'd been calling her since last week was an author who'd eventually become famous and respected?

The names were a slam to her pride when her own chances of even staying employed were looking slim.

She marched the rest of the way into the house, tossing her purse on a velvet-upholstered chair in the foyer, just as if this was her own home.

Thinking twice, she backed up and retrieved it.

"Going to bed already?" he asked.

"I'm tired."

"You're pissy."

She stopped in her tracks and glanced behind her. "Excuse me?"

He was hanging his hat on a rack as if he had all the kick-around time in the world to poke at her.

"I'm just saying that you're in a mood, Margot."

"Do you maybe think it's because you acted like a possessive troglodyte back at the bar?"

His eyebrows shot up as he sauntered nearer to her. "You do have a way with words."

Why wouldn't he outright engage in a sparring battle? It was the only comfortable way she knew to communicate with him.

He walked right by her, out of the foyer and into the family room, where he grabbed a remote for the big-screen TV, dropped down onto the sofa and turned on the device. A drop-down menu revealed shows that he had recorded, and he chose one.

Of all the programs in existence, Leigh's "Come-On Down Kitchen" appeared on the screen.

"You don't really watch this," Margot said, wandering to the room's entry and lingering there. Maybe she could start a fight with him yet.

"I recorded Leigh's show because I thought you and Dani might want to see the newest episode." He glanced at her. "Do you wanna?"

Even though his question was tipped with innuendo, she thought that he might be offering an olive branch of sorts, inviting her to relax with him.

Heck. She wasn't really that tired, anyway, so she found a good spot in the corner of the cozy sofa, far enough away from him to make a point.

Clint clearly thought it was amusing.

"Get over it, Margot," he said, reaching over, wrapping an arm around her and pulling her closer to him until her thigh was flush against his.

It took her a second to get her breath back. Took her a moment to get over how sexier-than-hell that move had been.

"This is way better," he said, sounding content.

Margot couldn't think of a thing to say. She merely attempted to control her heartbeat while they watched Leigh on the screen in her softly lit country kitchen, which boasted gingham curtains, evening-shaded trees peeking through the windows and the ingredients for a sensual Southern version of red velvet cake—emphasis on the velvet part—spread out before her on the counter. She was wearing a flannel shirt with one more button undone than she would've had in real life, flashing some cleavage and a little bit of tight tummy, since she had her shirt knotted at the bottom.

Being this close to Clint had Margot's adrenaline pumping, running hot and cold. Sitting next to him with his leg against hers was…different. Especially since she kept expecting him to make a bigger move.

She tried to breathe. *In, out. Don't be too loud about it. Just breathe.*

And she was doing okay until he did make a bigger move—if you could call it that.

He slipped an arm on the back of the sofa behind

her, and she could feel the vibration from his skin on the back of her neck.

A first date, she thought. That's what this felt like.

The date they'd never had before skipping to all the other parts.

They'd seen each other naked, felt each other come to orgasm and, suddenly, she realized that she wanted something else.

A quiet date moment like this, on a sofa, just sitting around with a person who made something come alive in your chest.

Not allowing herself to think too much about that buzzing sensation—if she did, she would only run—she sank back into the sofa a little bit, against his muscle-bunched arm.

Relax, she thought.

But, naturally, she couldn't.

Hell, she couldn't even follow Leigh's show, as her friend spread the red velvet batter in a cake pan with smooth strokes.

All Margot could do was think over and over again that Clint had his arm around her, and that she felt just like a teenager, anxious about the end of the night.

But then she started getting restless.

Time to go.

Time to run before it's too late.

By the time Leigh was making a batch of sinful cake frosting on the TV, Margot was a complete bundle of nerves, wondering if Clint was going to kiss her…and wondering if he wasn't.

Finally, she couldn't deal anymore.

"Mind if I watch the rest of this later?" she asked, standing up and away from him.

Far, far away.

If he was surprised, he didn't show it. "Be my guest."

"Thanks." She started to leave, but more words wanted to trip off her tongue.

She let them. "I mean, thanks for everything. It really was a good night."

And she made herself leave before she tripped herself, falling right into his arms.

MARGOT DIDN'T ACTUALLY sleep until dawn, when she heard the door shut downstairs, indicating that Clint had left for the working part of the ranch.

Finally, she thought, her eyes closing. No more wondering if he would come to her room to finish off all the building sexual tension from last night.

She went to sleep so quickly that she didn't even have time to feel disappointed.

A few hours later, when her smartphone alarm went off, she sprang up in bed, automatically bending down and dragging her purse by the straps across the floor, then plunging her hand inside to turn off the wake-up-lazy-bones chimes.

Right away, she dialed a number.

After the pick-up, Margot blurted out, "Dani?"

"Hey."

"He's got some nerve."

Dani paused on her end of the line, obviously trying to put two and two together. Then she laughed. "I know what you're saying really isn't funny, but it just sounds like you're a character from *Bye Bye Birdie*. You know, at the beginning when all the screwy teenagers are blabbing on the phones about all the romantic gossip and—"

"Dani."

"Okay, what did Clint do this time?" Then she halted.

"Wait. How could he be getting on your nerves if you're at home and not on his ranch?"

Time to come out with it. "I'm, uh, still here."

"What?"

She'd gotten called out yet again. "I didn't want to bother you with my issues when you and Riley were having worse ones."

"I *like* your issues, Marg. Believe me, they've been the highlight of my week." She didn't go into detail but instead asked, "Why did you decide to stay there?"

Here came the grilling, but it was a relief to get everything off her chest. "Clint had this idea for a new book."

"Oh, a book. How could I not have guessed that? I'm sure you and Clint have had a lot of literary discussions."

"I kid you not, Dani." And she described his idea.

Dani seemed to chew on it for a second. Then, "I would totally read that."

"You read everything I write, anyway."

"That's because your life has always been a vicarious pleasure."

Why did she sound so wistful?

Margot didn't have time to analyze the remark before Dani went on, in a much cheerier tone.

"You must be working very hard on that book, Marg. How late did you stay up last night *working?*"

"You're mocking me about this?" Margot swung her legs over her mattress, her toes skimming the floor. "I called to tell you how much he's driving me up a wall. I need a friendly ear."

"Then talk away."

So she related everything about her and Clint's time in the bar—the near kiss, the territorial way he'd kept

the other cowboys from dancing with her, even the end
of the night when it'd felt so much like a date.

Dani sighed. "Like this is all a surprise. Riley said…"

She dropped the sentence midway, and Margot
wasn't about to let that go.

"What did Riley say?"

Dani made an I'm-shutting-up-now sound. "Ignore
me. I really shouldn't have brought it up."

"Well, you did."

"Why do you even care when you're just going to
take off from the ranch soon? Unless…"

Oh, God. Even Dani suspected that Margot was
much more interested than she should be.

"Listen," Dani said. "I like Clint, and I know you,
Margot. And as long as I've known you, you freak out
at the first sign that a guy wants to get serious."

Margot lowered her voice. "Riley told you that Clint
wants to get serious?"

"I didn't say that."

"Say *something*." Anything.

Dani was definitely serious herself now. "I shouldn't
be the one saying something here. *You* say something.
You tell me why Clint has enough power to make you
call me in the morning bitching about him."

If Margot didn't know any better, she would've said
that the new Dani had done more than have a slight
physical makeover. She had a new way of dealing with
everyone, too.

Drawing her knees up and pulling them toward her
as she sat on the mattress, Margot knew that the time
for hemming and hawing was over with Dani.

And with herself, too.

"I have no clue what's going on," she said. "Last
week, I was this fabulous single girl on the go. This

week…" She closed her eyes, opened them. "This week I'm starting to think about what it'd be like to stay."

"With Clint?"

"Jeez, I can't believe I said that." Could she take it back?

Dani's tone gentled. "You're scared to death, aren't you? It's okay, Margot. Love's darn scary. It's hard to figure out."

You should know, Margot thought, wondering just how far Dani and Riley had mended the small tears in the seams of their relationship.

Her heart had started to palpitate way back at the mere mention of love. "Maybe we shouldn't say the *L* word. I can't even…"

"All right. Can I say *like* instead? Because you do like Clint, don't you?"

Margot hugged her knees even tighter. "I wish I didn't."

"But you do." There was some hope in her tone.

"Don't you dare tell Riley, because guys gossip just as much as girls. They just do it in far fewer words."

"I'll be mum about it. But what're you going to do?"

She shook her head. "I don't know." Then, after a hesitation, she slumped. "Nothing. I know I'm not going to do a damned thing, because this is a good fling, but otherwise…"

"Ah." Dani sounded disappointed.

But why shouldn't she be when Margot had no idea what it was like to be with someone in a normal relationship and would most likely blow an opportunity for one, anyway?

She shouldn't have called Dani. She shouldn't have even opened this can of worms, because what else did she have to give besides seventy-plus more slips of paper in a basket?

Nothing, she realized, thinking of her dead-end job, her restless, noncommittal spirit.

But maybe there was something after all, she thought, before saying goodbye to Dani.

She hadn't driven away from the ranch yet, and at least she could have one more night's worth of good times before she went back to whatever she had left.

AFTER A DAY full of training a quarter paint that he had bought last month, Clint returned to the house exhausted, headed for the shower.

The water's spray massaged his muscles and, of course, his mind went into fantasy mode, imagining that Margot wasn't in her room being a study bug and working on her project. Instead, she was here in the shower with him, running her hands over his body, soaping him up, easing him down from hours of labor.

It wasn't enough, though, and afterward, he went downstairs, thinking he would just throw a couple frozen dinners into the stove and see how much fight Margot had left in her when she came down to eat.

Would it be war?

Or would it be time to make up?

He found her waiting for him, sitting on a kitchen chair, her dark hair cascading over her shoulders as she wore that long white innocent-but-not-so-innocent negligee that he'd given her last weekend as a part of *his* basket.

As she smiled mysteriously at him, he nearly blew up.

Maybe she didn't notice, because she merely pushed a plate of meatloaf and vegetables across the table in his direction. She had food in front of her, too.

"I heard you come in," she said, "so I went ahead and warmed this up. I found some ground beef in the fridge earlier. Hope you don't mind."

"I don't," he said. "Thanks."

He wasn't sure what he was supposed to be doing with her sitting there in a sexy boudoir gown with meat-loaf on the table. Was he supposed to choose one or the other?

Was there a piece of paper he'd missed in her basket that had some kind of Hotsville, U.S.A., scenario written on it?

The only thing he knew for sure was that she was setting up another destination—their finale.

Let it play out, he thought. *Nothing earth-shattering is ever going to happen with her, anyway.* He shouldn't have even entertained the idea last night. Or ever.

Just imagine—successful city-girl Margot and him, the simple lone cowboy.

Sitting, he took a long drink of the water she also had waiting for him. The glass clinked with ice, and a slice of lemon decorated the top.

She slid a piece of paper over to him.

And there it was—a scenario from the basket.

He didn't read it yet, only looked at her for a moment as she gave him another cryptic smile.

A second or two ticked past, and he thought, *Why not?*

What did he have to lose?

As a small voice within answered, *Your heart?* he ignored it and read the paper.

Reykjavik ice bar, Iceland.

He glanced at her in that white negligee again. An ice princess. And, unfortunately, the image was more than just a role she was playing for the basket.

She was as cool as they came.

"It's a freezing place, this ice bar," she said. "When I went there, they gave me an actual ice cup for the cocktails. They also gave us parkas, so we wouldn't chill our butts off on the ice seats." She smiled, tracing a finger over the rim of her glass, which curiously didn't have water, just ice cubes. "The bar was a great place to find someone who could warm a girl up afterward."

He tightened his hand around his glass and spoke before he could think straight. "I don't want to hear about how you got warmed up."

A pause.

A heavy thud of time during which she was probably thinking that she had him wrapped around her little finger.

For a second, he believed that she might drop the basket game altogether, but then she reached into her glass, taking out some ice.

She stood and started walking out of the room, though not before saying, "Dinner can get cold for all I care, but you might want to come and warm *me* up."

Then she left.

Clint told himself to stay put. To not give in this time, because if he did, it'd be for real.

He didn't know if he could take another night with her, pretending it didn't matter anymore.

But then he found himself standing, walking out of the kitchen and into the hallway, drawn to her.

Always drawn to her.

He saw her in the hall, disappearing into the study, the lights doused inside. She looked like a ghost or...

Or a bride in that long negligee.

But he wouldn't dare tell her that, because he suspected it would ruin the last night they had together.

And he wanted it to be special, to be different.

Dammit, how had he gotten to this point? And why did it feel like he should've arrived much sooner?

He went to the dark room where he knew she was waiting, and the summer scent of her led him deep inside, even though he couldn't see anything but the faint white outline of her gown. He knew the reason she wanted darkness—it would make him wonder where the ice would touch his skin.

"Come here," she said.

She didn't call him "stud" now. Was that a good sign?

Telling himself that it was, he walked forward.

"Take off your shirt." Her voice cracked a little, or maybe he was just imagining that.

As he went along with her, he said, "Where's this going, Margot?"

"You'll see."

He hadn't been talking about this scenario. He'd meant something much bigger and, if she knew that he'd just laid himself on the line, she didn't acknowledge it. Instead, he felt her ice-dampened fingertips on his chest, and he started, shocked by the wet charge of the contact.

He caught her hand. "What happens after tonight?"

"I go back to my place." She tried to pull away.

But he wasn't letting go. "Why do I get the feeling that you don't want to go?"

"Are you going to talk all night long?"

His heart kicked at his chest. "Maybe I should. Maybe this is the best time to tell you that I don't want you to go, even though that's how you apparently operate."

"Just be quiet."

This time, when she touched him with an ice cube,

it was more aggressive. She slid it around his nipple, and he sucked in a breath.

Is she really all ice? he thought.

And he wondered if he would ever be able to melt her all the way.

She was doing a hell of a job of melting *him*. His blood was turning into blasts of steam as she kept tracing patterns on him with the slick cube.

Water ran down his chest, over his stomach, cool and tingling.

"Thatta boy," she whispered, easing her fingers into the waistline of his jeans.

Gripping her around the wrist again, he stopped her from going further with the ice. Then he released her and backed away.

"No more games, Margot. No more bubble baths or paintings or ice."

She laughed carelessly, just as she always had during their basket time together.

He forged ahead, still in the dark, wishing he could see her face. "Last night at the bar, I didn't want another man even looking at you. You know why? Because when I think of you being with anyone else, it drives me insane. Even after one damned week, all I want to do is be around you, smell your perfume, have you next to me in bed or on the sofa or wherever it is, just so you're there. You've already become a part of my home. Don't you realize that?"

She'd gone quiet, but he was going to make this night part of their history, erasing the one that had started everything off so badly in college.

Deliberately, he stepped forward until he felt just where she was, his skin singing at the proximity of her. Then he reached out with both hands, instinctively knowing where to cup her face.

He brushed his thumbs over her cheekbones, bending down so that he was nose to nose with her.

Her breath came quick against his lips.

"You belong *here,* with me," he whispered before kissing her softly, a touch of his mouth to hers.

A hint of the tenderness from him that had always been hiding just below the surface.

She made a protesting sound in her throat, dropping the ice and circling her fingers around his wrists as he palmed her face. But when he deepened the kiss, parting his lips just slightly, she seemed to lose form beneath him, her knees giving out.

He wrapped an arm around her, keeping her steady while pressing her to him at the same time, his other hand going to the back of her head.

When she sighed against his mouth—this sound one of pleasure—he restrained himself.

A real first kiss.

A gentle one that wasn't about sex or animal instinct.

This was about showing her how he felt without having to tell her and scare her off completely.

They kissed for what felt like hours, her mouth opening under his as they drew at each other, seeking, necking like two desperate kids who couldn't stand the thought of ever being apart.

She clung to him, her hands roaming his back as she kept making those urgent yet sweet sounds low in her throat.

When he finally lost the ability to breathe, he came up for air, still pressed against her, still holding her.

"No games," he said against her mouth. "This is

more real than what I've ever felt for anyone, Margot."

He waited for her to answer, every second like a drumbeat that would announce his fate.

12

THIS WAS MORE real than anything she'd ever felt.

And it frightened Margot to her very core.

As a pulse beat rapidly in her temples, speeding up her thoughts until she couldn't latch on to a single one of them, she realized that she'd been gripping Clint's waist.

She should say something. But what? Because telling him that she felt the same way about him would be a commitment, and she didn't do those. She'd made a career of hopping from one place to another, never staying, never wanting to.

Until he'd come along, offering her the first true home she'd ever had.

Making her realize that this…and him…were all she'd ever been looking for.

But he didn't understand that homes never lasted. They were way stations, just like people were way relationships. Homes broke down, sometimes with fatal consequences, and she was fine all by herself.

Always had been, always would be.

She wanted to flee now, even as he held her, warm, strong.

"Margot," he whispered, touching her cheek. "Don't leave me hanging."

Finally, she snatched a thought out of the spinning cycle of her mind. "I don't mean to."

"Good. Because I don't regret telling you how I feel. What I would regret is seeing you drive off, knowing that there was a chance things could've been different."

"Is there a chance?" she asked quietly. It hardly sounded like her.

"Why wouldn't there be?"

She thought of the stripped-down words he'd bared to her, words about how she belonged here. Even if they were in the dark right now, he had lit her up temporarily.

She wished she were capable of doing the same for him. He needed someone who'd be there when he faced his brothers the next time, someone who wanted to see him win at everything he did in life.

She didn't want to let him down when he realized that she was just good at temporary, and that was all.

He was still stroking her cheek, conjuring those butterflies in her chest, the fluttering sensation she'd never felt before when someone cared about you.

But those wings also felt like fear, because what would happen when the butterflies got tired and stopped trying to fly? What if those butterflies weren't even real in the first place?

She yearned to touch his face in the dark, just as he was doing to her. She wanted to show him without those hard-to-say words that she was going to take this risk, put her heart out there, give it to him.

Yet she couldn't.

She was the joke this time, and she probably always would be.

When she pulled back slightly from him, his fingers stiffened, and he took them away from her cheek.

He knew she couldn't do this, didn't he?

"This is happening too fast," she said, avoiding the issue altogether. She wasn't going to let this go anywhere.

His laugh barely disguised what she thought might be an injury—one she'd inflicted.

"Is there a certain amount of time that we *should* be taking to—"

She wouldn't let him say "fall in love" or anything even close.

"I just need to think," she said, moving toward the crack of light at the doorway. "My head's scrambled. I just need…time."

You're what's scrambled, she thought. *And you have no idea how to fix yourself.*

"All right, Margot." He sounded…confident? Or was that another mask to hide his resignation? "You take your time."

He was letting her off the hook, and she wondered whether he had never meant all the things he'd said in the first place. If this was really all about getting her to fall for him, it would be the ultimate joke.

But something inside of her told her that wasn't the case at all.

Still, even if she were to go running back to him, jumping into his arms, it wouldn't last. It never did for either of them, so why should they think that the odds were in their favor this time?

She left the room, telling herself not to look back.

Only forward, just as she'd always done.

CLINT LET HER go, because keeping her in the dark with him wasn't going to solve anything. It wasn't going to make her feel something for him when she obviously didn't.

She had merely been letting him down easy, Clint thought, waiting until he heard her climb the stairs so he could finally get out of that study.

Afterward, he shut the door behind him, as if he could box away what had just happened in there. A dark stain was growing in him, heavy and lonely.

Why had he even said anything to her when he knew damned well how Margot was going to react?

Going to bed, he tried to sleep on it, but that didn't work. He ended up watching TV until he couldn't keep his eyelids open anymore.

In the morning, the TV was still on, sounding tinny and loud at a time when the dawn usually came on soft waves of color through his window.

But even the sunrise was lackluster today.

He pulled on a pair of jeans, then went to his door. When he opened it, he almost stepped on a piece of paper.

He picked it up, his heart already sinking.

Clint,
I couldn't sleep, and since I was going to leave early in the morning, anyway, I thought I would just get out of your hair sooner rather than later.
    I owe you a big thanks, not only for your hospitality, but because you do know how to show a girl a good time. I'm never going to forget this past week, and I mean that.

Here, it was as if she'd stopped writing and started again. The penmanship was a little shakier.

Dani and Riley kept telling me that you'd changed since college, and they were right. You can do anything, Clint, and I'm not just blowing smoke at you. Some girl is going to be damned lucky to have you someday. She's going to be the type who doesn't have neurotic issues. She's going to be country through and through, and she's not going to be a fish out of water in your life. She's truly going to be perfect for you, and I wish you all the happiness in the world with her. She'll be the luckiest woman.

His gaze couldn't focus on the rest, which looked like platitudes and thank-yous for having her as a guest.

The writer, he thought. The woman who couldn't tell him all this in person last night.

His gut churned as he crumpled up the letter and tossed it behind him while he went into the hallway, toward her room, throwing open the door.

All he saw was a neatly made bed, just as if no one had stayed there.

Just as if she had never come into his life and then left it in pieces.

But this was how it had always been meant to go, Clint thought. How could it have turned out any other way with two people who'd only been trying to find closure with a decade-old fantasy?

Blanking out his mind—and everything else—Clint went to work on the ranch, driving to the horse barn, walking through it, feeling like an empty page.

His employees stared, but he barely felt it. And when

he got an email later in the day while he worked in the barn's office, all he could do was laugh.

It was from his brothers. They had stopped their threats and hired an attorney.

He leaned back in his chair, remembering what Margot had said to him at The 76 as they'd talked at the table by the dance floor.

I know someone who could help.

She'd been referring to a lawyer, but she'd had no way of knowing that the only person Clint longed to have at his side, fighting every battle with him, was her.

THE DAYS PLODDED by for Margot that week.

She tried to make them go faster by "filling her creative well," seeing as many movies as she could, reading like a freak and sorting through magazines to find some inspiration for a new project.

But she kept going back to daydreams about country bars, starlit nights, comfortable cowhide couches and a gazebo on a ranch.

And a cowboy who had messy golden hair, roguish blue eyes and a cocksure grin.

Even an early Sunday afternoon on her condo balcony with the newspaper and a plate of blueberry scones under the October sun couldn't cheer her up and out of this funk.

So she called the only two people who even had a chance of making her feel better.

First, she got Dani on the line for the conference call, then Leigh, who was shooting on location at a dairy, where she was going to make homemade ice cream in passion-laced flavors.

"Still hating myself," Margot said as soon as Leigh got on the line.

The Queen of Cream answered first. "Stop beating yourself up about Clint."

"Yeah," Dani said, a good friend until the end, although Margot knew she was frustrated with this romantic outcome. "You thought things weren't going to work out with him, so you nipped it in the bud."

And she'd nipped it with a letter. Margot heard it in every syllable her friends uttered.

She hadn't even been able to tell him what she really felt in person.

She rested her head on the back of the lounge chair. "I was afraid of what would happen if I tried to say those things to him face-to-face and not in a letter. There's a reason I'm a writer."

Or *was* a writer.

She still hadn't told Dani and Leigh about the canceled book or her bleak career outlook. Leigh was riding high, Dani was going to open her own business one day and Margot was deadweight.

Why did it seem as if Clint was the only person she could've confided in? He'd given her ideas, not commiseration.

He had made it seem as if they could find their way out of a dark room together, and with every day that passed, she wanted to believe that they might've made it if she'd decided she could break out of her patterns and change.

Too late, though, she thought. She'd already written the end to that story.

Leigh's sympathetic voice came back on. "What would you have said to him that you didn't write in the letter?"

She bit her bottom lip. "I have no idea how to put

what I feel into the words that come out of my mouth. And usually *those* words are the wrong ones, anyway."

"You know exactly what you should've said to him," Dani said.

Margot sat up. "What? That I'm all of a sudden so sure that I'm not going to get bored, just like my parents always did, or that he's not going to want to move on, either, like he always did?"

Dani piped in again. "That's what the Margot who won't get out of her rut would say. This Margot is scared to death."

"No, I'm…"

Yes, she was.

Leigh said, "When you love, you have to do it with everything you've got, right, Dani?"

"Right."

Dani sounded so sad that Margot's problems disappeared, and she seized the chance to get the spotlight off her. But she also did want to know what was going on with one of her very best friends.

"Is everything okay with you, Dan?"

On the other end of the line, she could hear her friend sigh.

"I mean it," Margot said. "We can go back to working my crap out later."

"Yeah," Dani finally said. "Of course we're okay. Don't change the subject."

A clump of silence passed before Dani said, "Okay, so it hasn't been such a smooth road. But Riley's been out of town on business, looking at some real estate for his boss, and he's coming back tonight. I'm going to give him a big welcome home. You should see the stuff I bought."

Margot got a bad feeling about this. "Stuff?"

"Uh-huh. We've got a cheeky little Boudoir-type place within driving range—tasteful but tempting. It would've been perfect for my auction basket if I'd had any imagination at the time."

Both Leigh and Margot went quiet until Margot said, "I'll be the first to tell you that fun and games in a bedroom aren't going to help anything."

"It'll put us both back in a good mood."

Dani's words echoed something Margot had said to Clint the night when things had first started spiraling out of control with Le Crazy Horse.

It was fun, okay?

But that had just been the half of it. It had been the first time she had been flailing with her feelings in the aftermath of sex. The first time she had done anything to avoid examining how she really felt about him.

She wasn't sure it was love. Not yet. But love started somewhere, and if this wasn't the beginning of it, she didn't know what else it could be.

Love. Her, Margot Walker, single girl on the go.

Now a true fish out of water.

Margot picked at a nylon lacing on her lounge chair. "Whatever you do, Dan, good luck."

"Tonight will be a great night for us. I'm sure of it. And, after his welcome home, I'll show him the wedding dress I finally ordered. I sent you all a picture of it this morning, so check your email."

Margot reached for her iPad on the glass-topped table next to her, accessing her account.

When the picture appeared, her heart seized up.

"It's beautiful, Dani."

Margot wasn't just saying that. The gown was simple, with a one-shoulder bodice, chiffon ruching and beaded flower appliqués. So Dani.

But, much to Margot's surprise, it could've been so her, too. Dressed in white, just as she'd been that last night with Clint in the negligee he'd given her. She sighed, and Leigh must've thought it was just because of the gown.

"Dammit, my phone's taking forever to download my email. Reception out here is terrible."

Dani laughed. "Don't worry—you'll see it later, crabby."

"I'm not crabby."

"But you are." Dani was in teasing mode now because the heat was off her. "I would be, too, if I still hadn't heard from my secret admirer."

"On that note," Leigh said, "I need to go. Everything's set for me to shoot."

They said their goodbyes, leaving Dani and Margot alone on the phone.

Margot said, "You did good, finding that dress."

"Believe it or not, sometimes I actually know what I'm doing." She had a wink in her voice. "You take care of yourself, okay? No maudlin nights, drinking wine, pining away for Clint."

Was that how Dani saw her these days? As a helpless thing who pined away?

She thought of Clint as waves of need—and the start of something bigger—rushed over her.

A single girl on the go. That's truly not who she was anymore, and maybe the readers who had been buying her books had seen that way before Margot had.

Clint had known it, too.

Getting up from her lounge chair, she went to the railing of her balcony, looking over the wide-open spaces that just didn't seem wide enough anymore—not after being on Clint's ranch.

It was time to travel someplace she'd never gone before, wasn't it? And even if she crashed and burned, at least she wouldn't have this hollow pit in the very center of her where Clint should be.

And that's when Margot decided that she hadn't been moving forward this past week—she'd been going nowhere.

Margot finally said to Dani, "No maudlin nights. I promise."

And after they hung up, she headed straight for her room, where her suitcases and travel gear were stored. She got one of her bags out of the closet and threw it on her bed.

She'd had enough of this. If she was going to travel, it needed to be in the direction she should've been heading all along.

BY THE TIME the headlights from Riley's truck flared over the family room windows of their rented suburban house, Dani was ready for him.

She took a deep breath, smoothing her hands down the negligee she'd purchased this week.

Egypt, she thought, feeling the sheer material beneath her hands. The beige gown didn't hide much, parting down the middle to show a flash of skin and belly button above the barely-there undies.

As she adjusted her headpiece—a chain of coins that dipped onto her forehead—she rushed to the hallway. But when she passed the mirror, she checked her makeup one last time.

Heavy eyeliner—check.

Red lipstick—check.

The front door opened, and she turned off the hall light, dashed to the bedroom, then lit a single candle on an end table. As the door closed, she took her place on the bed, her blood flowing hot as she made like Cleopatra and rested on her side, one hand propping up her head.

She heard a jangle of keys as Riley spilled them into the glazed ceramic bowl by the front door, then the sound of his footsteps on the wooden floor. Then...

The TV switching on?

She sprang up in bed, her headdress clinking. "Riley?"

A pause, then the TV volume going down. Footsteps into the hallway.

She got back into position.

"Dani? You home?"

"Yes, I am."

"The lights were off, so I—"

Then he stood in the doorway, the candlelight flickering over him. His eyebrows were knitted as he scanned the scene.

"Welcome to Egypt," she said, crooking a finger at him.

Her nightie covered one breast, but only with a teasing sheerness. The other breast was exposed as the material gaped away from her.

Passion clouded Riley's eyes, but she could see the sexual haze lift from them as the seconds passed.

She thought about how she'd lied to Margot and Leigh this morning. Things hadn't been so okay between her and Riley. He'd been on this business trip for most of the week, and before he'd gone, he'd spent a lot of time in the yard, mowing, cutting, weeding. She'd let him blow off steam out there, too, knowing they would sit and have another talk when he was ready.

But he hadn't been ready before he'd left town, so

she thought a little nudge might be in order. Plus, she'd missed him. Terribly.

She rolled to her belly. "I've been counting down the minutes until you got back."

"You know I have, too."

Why did he make it sound as if he'd been waiting until *she* got back from somewhere after leaving him behind?

"That's some getup," he said.

"I thought you might like a trip to an intriguing destination."

"Sounds like Margot and that basket of hers."

Another comment laden with deeper meaning. He was obviously referring to the way things between Margot and Clint hadn't turned out so well.

He came to sit on the bed, and her pulse darted up and almost out of her as she crawled over to him and started to unbutton his shirt.

"I did a lot of thinking while I was gone," he said.

She stopped with the buttons. Riley had always been a thinker—a stalwart man who never did something until he'd worked every angle out in his mind.

Why did she get the feeling that she'd been his main subject?

"You're about to say something bad," she said.

"No, Dani." He touched her headdress. "We were best friends before we were anything else, and I don't know if that set the tone for the rest of our lives. I should've expected change after being together for years."

"What do you mean?"

"I mean that what we felt for each other was always very straightforward and innocent. There were never wild nights like Margot had with Clint, where things

were stormy and crazy. I think that seeing them together did something to you, and I can't blame you for
that. You're only human." He ran a hand down her hair.
"But there're deeper things going on with you, too, and
that's what we have to work through before we set foot
in front of any wedding altar."

But we're Dani and Riley, she wanted to say. *Things
never go wrong.*

She took off the stupid headdress. "I don't want to
talk about my parents again and how they've warped
me."

He didn't say anything for a moment, but he finally
nodded. He wouldn't talk about it now, she thought,
even though it was clearly on his mind.

He took her headdress, handing it back to her. She
refused it.

"You think I'm rejecting you or something?" he
asked.

"Aren't you?"

"God, Dani. When I saw you lying here, I wanted to
tear off what little you have on."

"So why didn't you?"

He smiled. "Because I didn't choose you just for sex.
I'm going to spend the rest of my life with you, and
we're not going to work things out by going to Egypt."

He was right. Margot and Clint had found that out
the hard way, so why had she started down the same
path with Riley?

"You know what we need to do?" he asked.

She motioned to her costume. "Ask for a refund?"

With great tenderness, he kissed her, just a touch of
his lips on hers.

Just a world of exploding hearts and a shower of need
that twirled through Dani.

"We need to get to know each other all over again," he said, his fingers at her nape, his thumb caressing the sensitive spot near the center of her throat.

She made a small sound of pleasure. "I'd say you already know a lot about me."

"I think I know enough to realize that you want some excitement. And before we get married, I want you to get it all out of your system so you can't say we never tried this and we never tried that before we settled down."

It took her a moment to realize that this was Riley speaking. Her Riley.

"We're going to experiment?" she asked.

"You can put it however you want. I look at it as courting—getting to know you all over again."

"Courting." She laughed. "It's so…"

"Old-fashioned? Probably. But I can put old-fashioned behind if that's what you want."

Now she gaped at him. "What are you saying?"

There was a hint of something she'd never seen in Riley's gaze before, and it excited the heck out of her.

No—the *hell* out of her.

"I want you to show me everything about yourself, Dani, no matter what it is," he said. "Court me in whatever way you want."

Her imagination started to go berserk, as if Riley had opened a door to a room that she'd always kept locked, especially from him.

But he'd found a key.

He put the headdress back on her, that dark and sparkling gleam still in his gaze.

Dani smiled, feeling reborn.

And tonight, she was an Egyptian goddess with a servant who would do anything for her.

Anything and more.

13

THAT NIGHT, CLINT slammed the old-model push-button phone in his barn office into its cradle, letting the curses fly.

Luckily, nothing but the whicker of his stabled cutting horses answered him.

He'd just been trying to get a hold of his brothers, who'd left a message a few days ago while Clint was working, saying that their lawyer would finally be contacting Clint's own attorney this coming week for a meeting about Dad's will and the ranch.

Neither of them had answered any of his calls, so Clint hadn't even gotten the opportunity to talk some sense into them—not that they had ever listened to sense before. Hell, he didn't even have a lawyer yet. Good God, deep down, he had believed that his brothers would never go that far.

His own blood.

Yet they had, and the betrayal made Clint feel as if he'd been sideswiped by a car while sitting at a stop sign. He'd seen it coming in the rearview mirror, but he hadn't thought it would hit him.

Then…*CRASH*.

He shoved out of his chair, walking out of the sparse office and into the barn itself, his boots crunching over straw. The horses peered at him out of their stalls, and one, a favorite broodmare he called Calamity Jane, neighed at him.

It was as if she knew that he was upset about more than just his brothers. They were simply the topping on the mountain of hurt that was mostly Margot, who had also sideswiped him. And she had kept right on going down the road without ever looking back to see what kind of damage she'd inflicted.

He thought he'd be okay, but the injury had run deeper than he'd first realized. And it had only grown, day by day. Truthfully, he'd hung up the phone about a hundred times when he'd been about to call her, to ask her why she'd left that letter and nothing else.

He went to Calamity Jane, resting his hand on her muzzle as she canted her ears forward.

"I knew it all along," he said softly to her. "They all break your heart at some point. I just didn't believe it'd happen to me."

Jane sympathetically blinked her big brown eyes, as if telling him, "You can't lose hope."

God, he didn't want to let hope go. In his dreams, he kept imagining that Margot would appear one night in his room with her basket in hand, smiling, offering it to him so he could choose another destination. And when he read the slip of paper, it would say "Right here on this ranch, just outside Visalia, California."

But he would go anywhere for her, really.

Clint patted Calamity Jane. "She has no idea that I'd hop on a plane to the far corners for her. I never got the chance to tell her that."

She rubbed against him in solidarity just before he walked away, down the barn's aisle, where one of the ranch hands, a guy they called Blume, was mucking out a stall.

They said good-night, and Clint walked through the unseasonably warm evening, hopping into his truck and driving home.

His silent home with the dimly lit windows.

In the shower, he occupied himself with thoughts of what he would have for dinner, or if he should go out with the boys tonight, but he couldn't get excited about either one.

Still, he had to eat, so he put on a pair of sweats and a T-shirt, heading for the second-story hallway.

But then…

He thought he heard a voice outside the window that he'd cracked to let in some of the Indian summer night air.

Stunned into stillness, he listened again. It'd sounded like Margot.

But didn't he hear her voice and see her face in his thoughts all the time?

Just as he was about to write off the sound, he heard a pounding knock on his front door, then his doorbell rang.

"Clint! I know you're in there!"

He had to be hearing things.

He was almost afraid to go to his window and look down below, because if he was wrong—if he was just imagining this—he'd officially be crazy.

But he was pulled to that window, anyway, and he held his breath, his blood tapping as he opened the window all the way and leaned out.

And there she was, coming out from under the porch

eaves as if she'd heard the window creaking open, her hands on her hips.

Just as knee-weakening as ever under the porch light.

Her hair was piled at the nape of her neck, as if she'd haphazardly shoved it there, and she was wearing a long summer dress, as if she'd been lounging and had suddenly roused herself for a road trip.

He still couldn't believe it, but she seemed just as flabbergasted at the sight of him, her hands slipping down off her hips.

"Margot?" he asked, his voice raw.

It was obvious that she was trying to gather herself. "I…I just drove, and I ended up here for some reason."

For some reason. Had he been right to keep hoping…?

Pride and that all-too-present hurt came to his rescue, and it was as if a wall went up around his heart. He wasn't going to let her do this to him again.

"Did you forget something in the house?" he asked. "Your toothbrush? A pair of boots? Maybe a letter?"

She hung her head for a moment, then looked back up at him. "I didn't know what else to do, Clint."

"About what?"

"Are you going to make me yell everything up at you?"

He could either give her a hard time or he could hear her out.

But once she was inside his home, he wasn't sure he could ever let her out again.

Then she tilted her head. "I have a lot to say, Clint. Please."

And that was all it took to get him to fold. Dammit.

"Door's open," he said.

She glanced up at him for a few seconds longer,

and he could see that it had taken all her bravery to be here—just as it had for him when he'd put himself on a limb the last time they'd seen each other.

After she disappeared under the eaves, he heard his front door open. Then close.

Raking back his hair with his hand, he couldn't get his feet to move.

What if everything between them collapsed tonight? What if it'd never been there in the first place?

He couldn't stand more heartbreak—not after Margot's letter. Not after his brothers.

As he heard her footsteps, he finally got himself going, coming to stand by the top of the stairs.

She was at the bottom, gripping the polished rail.

And there they waited, so close but so far.

"You had a long trip," he finally said.

"I drove most of the day." She tightened her hold on the rail. "I would've driven a lot longer, though."

"For what, Margot?"

She hauled in a deep breath, blew it out. During that short space of time, he swore his heart banged at least fifty times.

"I couldn't stay away from you," she said. "I kept waking up at night, with the condo so quiet. I wished I could hear you breathing next to me, just like that one night we spent together." She laughed sadly. "I kept wondering what might have happened if I'd stayed another day with you. Then another, until they all just ran into each other in one long, happy time. Because, just like you said, this is more home than I've ever had, Clint, and it had everything to do with you."

Her emotion struck him, and he could barely get the words out. "And why didn't you just tell me that face-to-face?"

"Because I thought that if I had to say goodbye in front of you, I wouldn't have done it."

Shaking his head, he almost gave up. Sometimes she made no sense.

But, God help him, most of the time he actually understood her nonsensical thoughts—just like now.

"I was so wrong," she said. "That's why I'm here, to tell you everything that was written between every line in that letter." She took the first stair, pausing on it. "I told you that you'd find another girl who was perfect for you, when all along I knew that she might be me. I've always done the leaving, and I couldn't stand the thought of what might happen if I got in too deep with you and you someday left me."

As he watched, she climbed up two more steps, and his blood gave a push in his veins.

"Why would you think I'd leave?" he asked.

She clutched the rail. "Mainly because you seem to think I'm this successful woman, and in the near future, when you inevitably found out that I'm not anymore, you were going to change your mind about me."

"What are you talking about?"

"My writing career is going down the tubes." She tensed up, as if anticipating his make-or-break reaction.

"Are you kidding?" he said.

She gave him a puzzled glance.

"Margot," he said, coming down one stair, "you're the last person in the world who'd ever be a failure."

It was as if the air had cracked between them, tumbling down.

She lowered her head, her voice thick. "You're the only one I've told about this. And that has to say something, doesn't it? That you're the one I trusted to hear it when, not too long ago, I didn't trust you at all?"

He walked the rest of the way to meet her on the stairway, and when he did, he slipped his hand under her chin to make her look up at him. Her eyes were shiny from unshed tears.

"You don't know," he said, "just how gratified I am to be the one you told."

She bit her lip, then nodded, holding on to his arm instead of the railing now.

He touched her jaw with his fingertips, hardly believing this was happening.

"I came back to offer more than an apology and explanations, though," she said. "First, I want to be here when you have to deal with your brothers."

At this, his throat tightened up. He could give her a home, but she gave him the support he'd always wanted, though he'd never realized it until now.

They'd been drawn to each other in college, but it'd taken years of living to make their connection come alive, giving each other what they really needed.

She wasn't done. "I want to be that fish-out-of-water, true country girl who lives where your parents lived so happily. And, well, this next one proves just how superficial I am, but I want to show everyone that the joke's on them."

When he took her into his arms, she fit against him as if she was made to be there and nowhere else in this world.

"Just imagine," he murmured into her hair. "Two butts of a joke who ended up together."

Then he brushed his lips over hers, more gently than any touch they'd ever shared. But it was enough to zing a sizzling thrill over and through every inch of him.

Without having to say anything, they sank to the

stairs, him taking her weight on his body as he cradled her against him.

He worked his fingers at her nape, undoing that bundle of hair until it tumbled down, thick and fragrant. He kept kissing her—little pecks at the corner of her mouth, on her cheek, under her jaw, making her take in tiny breaths.

The first time they'd been together at the reunion, he'd told her he would find eighty ways to pleasure her, but he hadn't known about these innocent, erotic places before. Now, each one was a discovery in itself.

A kiss to the neck, and she gasped.

A nip at the skin between her collarbone and shoulder, and she clutched at his T-shirt.

Then back to her mouth—lush, devouring, slow and easy.

They made out on the stairway, her body stretched over his, for what seemed like hours. Just kissing like famished kids and nothing else.

Until she slid her hand under his shirt, her palm on his ribs.

He cupped her face, looking into her pale, clear eyes. "You don't want to take it a little slower this time?"

Because now, it wouldn't be a basket game.

She looked at him, *into* him. "I want all of you, all the time, Clint."

And she kissed him again, taking them into their own world.

MARGOT MEANT EVERY word. She'd driven for miles and miles to say them, stopping only once for gas and taking off again, and the entire time, her heart had been in her throat.

What was she going to say?

Was he going to kick her out, tell her she'd had her chance and she'd blown it?

But he'd accepted everything about her, even the parts she'd been so afraid to expose to anyone.

The *Cosmo* girl and the cowboy. Who would've ever called it?

He rolled her to the side, keeping her in his strong arms, until she grasped the bottom of his T-shirt, yanking it up and over his head. Unable to wait a moment more, she pulled down the top of her dress, where the basic white bra she'd put on this morning pressed against her breasts, making them swell.

"I didn't have time to change clothes," she said, as if in apology for the least exotic wardrobe possible.

She drew in a breath as he kissed the tops of her breasts.

This was no basket-inspired costume, but he didn't seem to mind.

"I'll change your clothes for you," he said, reaching around her back to unhook her.

Her breasts spilled out, and he smiled, positioning her above him so that he could take her into his mouth, suck on her until she wiggled on top of him, plumped and damp between her legs.

He slipped a hand under her dress, pressing against her achiest spot.

"You have way too many clothes on, anyway," he murmured.

Then he tugged her dress up, over her head, just as she'd done with his T-shirt.

"And these?" he said, pulling at her panties. "No need for them, either."

She braced herself on the steps as he worked the material down her legs and off her body.

Then he placed his hands on her ribs, guiding her so that her most vulnerable area was above him, her hands braced on the steps, her legs open for him.

Being this exposed caused her pulse to hammer, and he made her wait, no doubt teasing her, just as he'd always done.

And always would, if she had her way about it.

"Here's a place I haven't kissed today," he said, using his fingers to part her.

She held back a delighted sound, and he laughed, knowing what he did to her.

But instead of taking that as a devilish move in one of their games, she accepted it, took it wholeheartedly, then lowered her hips to him.

He kissed her thoroughly, with mouth and tongue. Slow laves, maddening sucks, licks and pulls. All the while, heat gathered in her belly, wisps curling up and up until she almost felt carried away.

"Don't come yet," he said, guiding her down his body so that she could rub herself against the bulge in his sweats, feeling his tip.

"I'm not sure I can wait," she whispered.

"Now who's the one who's not going to last?"

Le Bain. She'd taunted him about coming too soon when they'd been in that bubble bath together.

Her cowboy. Her Clint.

He took off the sweats, revealing his erection.

"Don't worry about what comes next." She touched him. "I'm on the pill, and—"

He assured her that he was fine, too. He'd barely even gotten the words out before he eased into her, so gently that she could feel every sliding inch.

They didn't move for a moment, just looked into each other's eyes.

She saw something so profound there that pressure built in her chest this time, not only in her belly.

A future. Their future.

He moved inside her, tender thrusts, the sweat of their bodies making them slip against each other. When he turned her over, his arms under her as a cushion, he pounded into her, pushing her up the stairs.

Up...up...

She was ascending in more than one way, climbing to a spot that made everything so clear, so new, so—

Her climax buffeted her, a million wet splashes, like a storm that had thrashed out of her and into him, because he came right after her.

And then, when they both had calmed a little, instead of trying to think of a way to escape him before he could look into her eyes again, she stared into his gaze.

She allowed him to see all the way into her for the very first time.

Epilogue

WITH HALLOWEEN JUST around the corner, Clint and Margot had decorated the ranch house with carved pumpkins and ghoulies like paper ghosts that hung from the corners of the family and living rooms.

He stood next to a life-size skeleton that Margot had unearthed from the storage room after she'd moved her stuff into the house.

"Is this really suitable for a housewarming?" he asked her as she fluffed the hair of a broomstick-bound witch near the fireplace.

"I think our guests have seen scarier things," she said, coming over to him and cuddling into his side.

He wrapped an arm around her—his fledgling cowgirl in jeans and a fashionable rodeo shirt. It wasn't a costume, either. It was just Margot, stripped down to her fish-who-found-water self.

He kissed her, long and easy. No rush, because they had all the time in the world.

But there was something beating at him nonetheless. Something he'd wanted to say to her for the past couple of weeks.

Nuzzling her ear, he went for it, whispering, "Margot…"

"I love you so much, Clint."

Warmth flooded him, here, there, everywhere. "You do?"

"I do." Her eyes were wide, as if this were the most momentous thing that had ever happened to her.

He must've taken too long to return the sentiment, because she gave him a little push on the chest.

"Well, do *you*?" she asked.

"Hell. Yeah." He laughed, drawing her back into his arms. "You just beat me to saying it."

As they laughed together and Clint swung her around, the front door opened.

They didn't bother to pull apart, not these days, when the secret was out about them.

"Barbecue's ready." Riley's voice.

"Be right there." Clint picked Margot up, resting her like a sack of grain on his hip until she laughed even harder.

"This is how we wrangle women on a ranch," he said, carrying her until she wiggled so much that he had to put her down.

She pushed the hair out of her face. "Try that tonight, and I just might…"

"Do what?"

She shrugged, walking away from him toward the front door, giving her hips an extra shimmy.

"I just might rope *you* up."

"Promises, promises."

He chased her out the door to the back patio, where Dani was helping Riley at the grill and Leigh was walking around on the far lawn, holding a beer in one hand and a phone in the other.

As Clint sat next to Margot at the long table, in front of a selection of salads, brown-sugar franks and beans and honey-corn-bread muffins, Dani and Riley brought over the sauce-covered grilled ribs.

When Dani reached to the vegetable plate for a piece of celery, feeding it to Riley, Margot gave Clint a knowing glance.

The other couple was "courting" all over again. They still seemed on edge with each other sometimes, as if so much had happened since the beginning of the month that they couldn't quite get over it, but this was a start.

After all, they were Dani and Riley. They would find a way.

"Eat up," Riley said to Clint as Dani finished the rest of the celery. He put the ribs on the table. "You're gonna need strength for tomorrow."

Margot was already slicing her meat, with much gusto, Clint thought.

"Clint's brothers are the ones who need the protein," she said. "Our lawyer's going to put them through the wringer."

His brothers hadn't backed off from their strong-arming. But as Clint looked around the table, he realized that he'd found a far better family.

And someone even more special than that.

He kissed Margot again, and she sent him a saucy, confident grin. Being out in the country, starting her blog about a city-girl-goes-rustic lifestyle, had put color in her cheeks.

When Leigh came wandering back to the patio, all attention rested on her, especially because she had gone a little pale.

"What's wrong?" Dani and Margot asked at the same time.

"That was Beth Dahrling," she said, sitting in a chair at the end of the table. "The man who bought my basket is arriving back in the country next week. He's wondering when we can arrange our…"

Clint cleared his throat, saving Leigh from saying the rest of it.

Margot put down her knife. "Are you going to blow him off?"

Leigh took one good look at Margot sitting so closely to Clint, and she got a yearning glint in her gaze.

Was she wondering what a basket might bring her, too?

She reached for the asparagus with lemon pasta salad. "I'm going to tell him I'm available, and we're going to see what happens."

"Even though you have no idea who he is?" Margot asked.

Leigh hesitated, then nodded.

"Go, Leigh!" Dani said.

They all lifted their drinks in a toast.

"Go, Leigh!"

She still seemed wary at the prospect of this date as she toasted right back at them, but that longing remained in her gaze—something that disappeared only when she closed her eyes while taking a deep draught of beer.

Under the table, Margot squeezed Clint's knee. She'd seen Leigh's expression, too.

As he took her hand in his, entwining fingers, he thought about all the trips left in Margot's own basket.

And the many that they would be making up on their own as they went along.

* * * * *

COMING NEXT MONTH FROM

HARLEQUIN *Blaze*

Available July 23, 2013

#759 THE HEART WON'T LIE • *Sons of Chance*
by Vicki Lewis Thompson

Western writer Michael James Hartford needs to learn how to act like a cowboy—fast. But it isn't until he comes to the Last Chance Ranch—and falls for socialite-turned-housekeeper Keri Fitzgerald—that he really discovers how to ride....

#760 TO THE LIMIT • *Uniformly Hot!*
by Jo Leigh

Air force pilot Sam Brody has had his wings clipped. Now he's only teaching other flyboys. And his fling with the hottest woman on the base has taken a nosedive, too...because Emma Lockwood belongs to someone else.

#761 HALF-HITCHED • *The Wrong Bed*
by Isabel Sharpe

Attending a destination wedding is the *perfect* time for Addie Sewell to seduce Kevin, The One Who Got Away. But when she climbs into the wrong bed and discovers sexy yacht owner Derek, The One Who's Here Right Now might just be the ticket!

#762 TAKING HIM DOWN
by Meg Maguire

Rising MMA star Rich Estrada loves exactly two things—his family and a good scrap. But when sexy Lindsey Tuttle works her way into his heart, keeping his priorities straight may just prove the toughest fight of his life.

SPECIAL EXCERPT FROM

HARLEQUIN

Blaze

Enjoy this sneak peek at

Half-Hitched

by Isabel Sharpe, part of The Wrong Bed series
from Harlequin Blaze

Available July 23 wherever
Harlequin books are sold.

Addie Sewell held her breath as she headed for Kevin's room. *First bedroom on the right.*

Eleven years later, she'd feel that wonderful mouth on hers again, would feel those strong arms around her, would feel his hand on her breast. And so much more.

Addie reached for the handle and slipped into the room. *Done!*

She closed the door carefully behind her, listening for any sign that Kevin had heard her.

He was still, his breathing slow and even.

She was in.

For a few seconds Addie stood quietly, amazed that she'd actually done this, that she, Princess Rut, had snuck mostly naked into a man's room in order to seduce him.

A sudden calm came over her. This was right.

As silently as possible, she walked toward the bed. In the dim light she could see a swathe of naked back, his head bent, partly hidden by the pillow.

A rush of tenderness. Kevin Ames. The One That Got Away.

HBEXP79765

She let her sweater pool at her feet as she pictured Kevin hours earlier. Laughing with that Derek Bates and all the other wedding guests.

Totally naked now, heart pounding, she climbed onto the bed then slid down to spoon behind him. His body was warm against hers, his skin soft, his torso much broader than she'd expected. They fit together perfectly.

She knew the instant he woke up, when his body tensed beside hers.

"It's Addie."

"Addie," he whispered.

Addie smiled. She would have thought after all he had to drink and how soundly he'd been passed out downstairs, that she might have trouble waking him.

She drew her fingers down his powerful arm—strangely bigger than she expected. "Do you mind that I'm here?"

He chuckled, deep and low. Addie stilled. She'd *never* heard Kevin laugh like that.

Before she could think further, his body heaved over and she was underneath him, his broad masculine frame trapping her against the sheets. And before she could say anything, he kissed her, a long, slow sweet kiss.

When he came up for air, she knew she'd have to do something. *Say something.*

But then he was kissing her again. And this time her body caught fire.

Because it was so, so good.

Beyond good. Unbelievably good.

It just wasn't Kevin.

Pick up HALF-HITCHED by Isabel Sharpe, available July 23 wherever you buy Harlequin® Blaze® books.

REQUEST YOUR FREE BOOKS!
2 FREE NOVELS PLUS 2 FREE GIFTS!

HARLEQUIN®

Blaze®

red-hot reads!

YES! Please send me 2 FREE Harlequin® Blaze™ novels and my 2 FREE gifts (gifts are worth about $10). After receiving them, if I don't wish to receive any more books, I can return the shipping statement marked "cancel." If I don't cancel, I will receive 4 brand-new novels every month and be billed just $4.74 per book in the U.S. or $4.96 per book in Canada. That's a savings of at least 14% off the cover price. It's quite a bargain. Shipping and handling is just 50¢ per book in the U.S. and 75¢ per book in Canada.* I understand that accepting the 2 free books and gifts places me under no obligation to buy anything. I can always return a shipment and cancel at any time. Even if I never buy another book, the two free books and gifts are mine to keep forever.

150/350 HDN F4WC

Name _____ (PLEASE PRINT) _____

Address _____ Apt. #

City _____ State/Prov. _____ Zip/Postal Code

Signature (if under 18, a parent or guardian must sign)

Mail to the **Harlequin® Reader Service:**
IN U.S.A.: P.O. Box 1867, Buffalo, NY 14240-1867
IN CANADA: P.O. Box 609, Fort Erie, Ontario L2A 5X3

Want to try two free books from another line?
Call 1-800-873-8635 or visit www.ReaderService.com.

* Terms and prices subject to change without notice. Prices do not include applicable taxes. Sales tax applicable in N.Y. Canadian residents will be charged applicable taxes. Offer not valid in Quebec. This offer is limited to one order per household. Not valid for current subscribers to Harlequin Blaze books. All orders subject to credit approval. Credit or debit balances in a customer's account(s) may be offset by any other outstanding balance owed by or to the customer. Please allow 4 to 6 weeks for delivery. Offer available while quantities last.

Your Privacy—The Harlequin® Reader Service is committed to protecting your privacy. Our Privacy Policy is available online at www.ReaderService.com or upon request from the Harlequin Reader Service.

We make a portion of our mailing list available to reputable third parties that offer products we believe may interest you. If you prefer that we not exchange your name with third parties, or if you wish to clarify or modify your communication preferences, please visit us at www.ReaderService.com/consumerschoice or write to us at Harlequin Reader Service Preference Service, P.O. Box 9062, Buffalo, NY 14269. Include your complete name and address.

HB13R2

This time, it's no-holds-barred!

Matchmaker Lindsey Tuttle always thought Rich Estrada was a whole lot of sexy. What's not to lust after? He's a gorgeous, flirty mixed martial arts fighter. When they find themselves heating up during an unexpected—and superintense—make-out session, Lindsey is ready...until Rich ends it with no explanation.

Almost a year later, with a broken foot, Rich is back in Boston before his next fight. But this could be the perfect time for a rematch with his sexy little matchmaker....

Pick up

Taking Him Down
by *Meg Maguire*

available July 23, 2013, wherever you buy Harlequin Blaze books.

Red-Hot Reads
www.Harlequin.com

SADDLE UP AND READ 'EM!

Looking for another great Western read? Check out these August reads from the PASSION category!

CANYON by Brenda Jackson
The Westmorelands
Harlequin Desire

THE HEART WON'T LIE by Vicki Lewis Thompson
Sons of Chance
Harlequin Blaze

Look for these great Western reads AND MORE available wherever books are sold or visit
www.Harlequin.com/Westerns